THE KAIROS BOXES

— Godstone —

by

G. A. Williams

**Grosvenor House
Publishing Limited**

G. A. Williams is hereby identified as author of this
work in accordance with Section 77 of the Copyright, Designs
and Patents Act 1988

The book cover picture is copyright to Susan Josephine Heyer Skinner

This book is published by
Grosvenor House Publishing Ltd
28-30 High Street, Guildford, Surrey, GU1 3HY.
www.grosvenorhousepublishing.co.uk

A CIP record for this book
is available from the British Library

ISBN 978-1-907211-29-4

'Godstone'

Book One of
'The Kairos Boxes'

By G. A. Williams

Cover Art by
Susan Josephine Heyer Skinner

'The Old Tree' (linocut print) by
Mark Morgan

Illustrations by
Alan Williams

To all those who have assisted me
in the creation of this book –

Thank you

What is time?
If no one asks me, I know;
but if any person should
require me to tell him,
I cannot.

– Augustine

Introduction

This book is not the story of one village, nor of one district, though even in the smallest of places, tales abound. Myth and legend mingle here with real history, with real characters brought into fictional possibilities.

'Godstone' is a journey through history, hinting at the future, a tale that spreads like ripples on the surface of a pond. It is a story which reaches out beyond the confines of the English countryside to far-off nations... and towards answers to its questions.

This is not a history book, but it contains much that is factual. Where real historical figures and places have been used, I have mostly kept them in their correct times and settings. However, for the sake of the story, this has not always been the case. For example Polly Paine (or Pain/Payne) was, it is recorded, an early nineteenth century woman and not a sixteenth century one. Legends about her make the claim that she had the ability to change into the form of an animal, notably that of a hare (or sometimes a dog). Bad events were said to have surrounded the appearance of the hare, causing the people of Godstone to finally hunt it down. It escaped the hunt, but wounded its leg and thereafter Polly Paine was seen to limp...

It is to two of the historical characters that I would like to dedicate this book. The most remarkable of people are often forgotten and barely known in their lifetimes. John Launder and Thomas Iveson (the 'Godstone Martyrs') were such people. To have stood up against the most terrifying opposition deserves respect and remembrance. (I would also like to honour the memory of the 'East Grinstead Martyrs', who do not feature in the story, although their town does.)

This book is dedicated to the 'Godstone Martyrs' and all of their kind, throughout the world and throughout time.

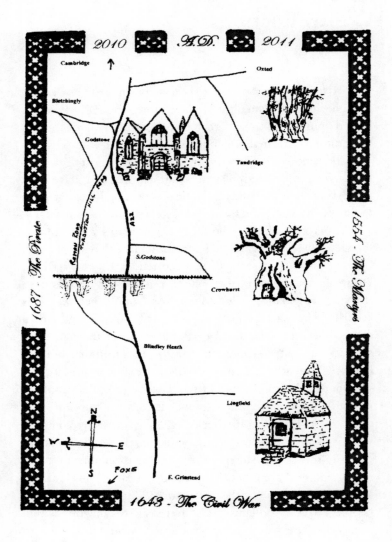

Contents

Chapter One

Jacob

Jacob knew there was more to life – not that his life was so bad, but there had to be more. At seventeen years of age, he was a prime target of that tyrant... fashion. Fashion: following the crowd, being cool, being like everyone else, or trying to imitate some god-like 'celebrity'. Yes, there had to be more.

He did make concessions to the tyrant, wearing some of those dreaded labels that magically turn clothing from the ordinary to the admirable. He did this to keep other people off his back. Being the odd one out is the vocation of the strong – and although not weak in character, Jacob didn't relish the battle... well, not all the time.

However, to Jacob, being uncool was the new cool, and after all, here in 2010, hadn't the geeks finally triumphed? The gods of sport and media, although doing alright, were now dwarfed by the computer generation. These titans of the new industrial revolution were the real players on the scene, and without even having to break a sweat.

The problem with not following the crowd was that he did not know which course his life should take. It had seemed alright, a few years before, to sit at the back of the class, his mind somewhere else, and wishing his body was as well. However, things were now getting serious. Increasingly important exams needed to be passed, and he had to consider career options. There was no more time for daydreaming.

Jacob wished that his parents were still around to guide him. Instead, it was his uncle who had brought him up. Though he had done his best, he hadn't always been the wisest of counsels. Not that his Uncle Andrew was lacking in the brain department – on the contrary; he was a university professor, and a notable one at that. It was probably from him that Jacob had inherited his individualistic streak.

His uncle was unusual in some ways; he didn't even own a television, reasoning that it polluted the mind. The lack of a television was surprising in light of the multitude of other media devices that cluttered the house, and yet more devices that to Jacob remained a mystery. The rambling old Victorian house in the village of Godstone was, it would be fair to say, in need of a woman's touch. However, it was very much home to Jacob. Its old and elaborate cast iron fireplaces with marble surrounds, oak dado rails and ornate cornicing stood in stark contrast to all the gadgetry scattered about.

Godstone, an ancient small village formerly known as Wolcnestede was once part of the realm of King Ethelred the Unready, a somewhat embarrassing title. Ethelred spent much of his reign trying to deal with Viking invaders, not very successfully. He did manage to see off King Canute for a while, who was not ready for... 'The Unready.' King Canute was, some say, the man who sat on a beach and tried to tell the tide to stop – strange times.

As with any old settlement, Godstone had had its fair share of notable events. In 1349, an unwelcome guest appeared in the village... the Black Death. It swept through, almost wiping the village out. The dead were buried on either side of 'Bullbeggars Lane' – men on one side, women the other. This terrible affliction wiped out between thirty and sixty percent of Europe's population.

Jacob had been made to study such dates, people and places sometime earlier for a local history project at school – unaware of the future relevance it would have for him. Another of these facts concerned 1554-55 and related to another notorious event. That was the arrest and death by burning of the 'Godstone Martyrs', John Launder and Thomas Iveson. Their crime had been to attend a service in which the English Prayer Book was used. Not much of a crime you'd think – but it was to Queen 'Bloody' Mary.

Now history was a real passion of Jacob's – after all, it was all about stories and surely, he considered, there had to be many exciting ones to be discovered since the genesis of man. He had always felt an affinity with the past and a wonder of the future, and not just because he'd watched Doctor Who (at someone else's house).

However, the present wasn't altogether without its fascinations. Rachel Isaacson was eighteen, slightly older than he. Though not much of an age gap, it was enough to make things harder for Jacob. She lived 'twelve doors down' and they had built a friendship travelling on the bus, to and from college. Rachel was different from most of the girls he knew, more serious. She knew her own mind, but not in an arrogant way. It was Rachel's maturity that made Jacob doubt that she would be interested in someone younger than herself, but the doubt wasn't enough to quench the hope.

Rachel was a member of the choir of the church of St. Nicholas. As in many an English village, this ancient place of worship was one of the centrepieces of the community, not yet replaced by the supermarkets. Beautiful countryside surrounded it, and there was a large pond nearby, home to a number of Canadian geese, moorhens and the obligatory ducks.

St. Nicholas' Church was soon to hold its annual Christmas carol service. It wasn't something Jacob would ordinarily be drawn to – however, he knew Rachel was going to be involved, and that gave him an incentive to attend. Jacob had told her at college that he would be going. She seemed happy about that, which encouraged him.

Jacob was open-minded on matters religious, at least as much as you can be when you've been brought up to believe all such things are nonsense. He hadn't been to church very much, mostly only with his old school, as his uncle didn't approve. "Fairy tales for the ignorant," he would say – "Science is all we need, Jacob, not the Sky Fairy". With Christmas approaching and Rachel's part in the carol service, he wasn't prepared to let his uncle's opinion get in the way on this occasion.

When it arrived, Christmas Eve 2010 was cold but, as most Christmases in England, not white. Those romantic snowy church scenes were mostly the preserve of greetings cards. Nevertheless, it felt good walking (to walk or to be walking) down the footpath from the centre of the village leading to St. Nicholas'. Despite not having much in terms of family to celebrate with, it was still his favourite time of the year. The St. Nicholas' church building may once have been the centre of the village – but after the plague had wiped out the original village, another had sprung up in Tudor times.

The Professor had been very busy in the time leading up to Christmas. He was out every night and strangely evasive when Jacob asked him what he had been doing. So, as it turned out, Jacob hadn't had to face any awkward, embarrassing questions about where he was going anyway. Jacob was happy about that, somehow feeling a need to impress his uncle. Perhaps it was because the Professor was his only living relative.

Jacob passed the 'Bay Pond' on his left and soon came to the end of the path that led into Church Lane. Before him now stood the St. Nicholas' church building, a large 13th century construction built at the location of an earlier Norman one. It was flanked on one side by the beautiful St. Mary's

Almshouses. Jacob enjoyed the sight, as he did all things historic, but would also quite have liked a castle near his home to complete the set.

Walking up the steps and through the lychgate, he entered the churchyard. Pausing briefly, Jacob thought about all those who had gone before him, down the centuries, to this place. Nearing the church doors, Jacob scanned the graves in the near darkness, trying to find the tombstone of the notorious pirate John Trenchman, complete with skull and crossbones emblem. Trenchman was said to have haunted the area after having been buried in 'unconsecrated' ground. That is, until he was reburied, with a full Christian service, in the St Nicholas' Church graveyard. Jacob, being certain (almost) of natural explanations for everything, didn't believe in ghosts. Nevertheless, he found it an interesting piece of local folklore.

He was greeted at the entrance by a smiling middle-class lady in her fifties who handed him a service sheet. The church building was three-quarters full and lit by candles, which added to the warm ambience. Finding an anonymous place to sit at the back of the building, but still in sight of Rachel, he sat down and looked at his service sheet self-consciously.

The congregation, a mixture of the faithful, the outwardly religious and those who wanted to feel 'christmassy' (if there is such a word), stood up and joined in the familiar choruses as the service began. Jacob glanced towards Rachel who was seated in the choir stalls. He thought to himself that her other potential suitors would probably be down at the 'Fox and Hounds' pub instead. The 'Fox' was also the place where the pirate Trenchman had died all those years ago. He had staggered there, mortally wounded, after having been ambushed by the King's men while on a smuggling trip with his gang.

A brief sermon followed, after a few more carols. Jacob had been only half listening, but he was brought to full attention when the vicar began to speak of prophecies in the Bible relating to the birth of Jesus Christ. He never realised such things were in the Bible and wondered at the possibilities of knowing the future, before succumbing to the scepticism that his uncle had driven into him. He supposed that somehow, these prophesies must have been inserted after the events. However, the vicar surprised Jacob by finishing with a challenge to the congregation – to test if what he had said was true and not just to take his word for it. This impressed Jacob and he decided to do just that... when he had the time.

The service ended, and he made his way through the contented throng to Rachel. They smiled at each other and exchanged greetings. Rachel actually did quite like Jacob; he was slightly better looking than average and, at about five feet and ten inches, a little taller than she was. More importantly to her, he was different to the other lads – more thoughtful, more considerate and in some ways old-fashioned. Maybe he wasn't quite the Mr Darcy of author Jane Austen's creation, but more Darcy than most – just a shame that he was younger than she was, she thought.

After Jacob and Rachel had finished their almost compulsory hot tea and mince pie, it was time to say goodbye. "Maybe we could go out sometime... to the cinema," he stuttered.

"Yes, maybe," she replied smiling. Jacob decided he'd better leave it at that and wished her a happy Christmas.

Outside the building, it had started to snow just a little. "This is too good to be true," he said to himself and felt like punching the air, but decided that he'd better not, as there were other people around. Turning back down the path, he made his way towards home. If Jacob felt he was having a remarkable Christmas so far, then he was to be amazed at what was about to follow.

Chapter Two

An Unusual Christmas

The exterior of number 87 Wigglesworth Road was decked out with clear light bulbs along the top of the ground floor windows (the Professor considered coloured ones 'downmarket'), whilst a Christmas tree took centre stage in the middle of the front garden. Inside the house, even some of the gadgetry had been tidied up and put away.

Normally, at the house of Professor Andrew Ketterley, there would be a number of guests for Christmas – friends only, as he was now divorced and Jacob was his only family – but not this year. The Professor hadn't arranged anything and had seemed totally preoccupied with some secret matter. Even his letters remained unopened, which was quite unusual for him.

It was Christmas morning and Jacob was in his bedroom wrapping up his uncle's presents – mostly science-related books and classical music albums. Not having a television, Jacob made do with watching DVDs on his laptop. The final battle scene of 'Prince Caspian' was just reaching its climax as he finished the last parcel.

Downstairs in the lounge, Jacob's uncle lit the log fire. They did have central heating, but he had always thought there was something extra-special about a real fire. Christmas can be a time for bringing back memories, and he thought back to some of the happier times with his ex-wife, pondering on how things might have turned out differently. He blamed himself for spending too much time in his work and realised that recently, he had fallen into his old habits.

"Happy Christmas, mate," he said as Jacob came into the room.

"'Mate'? That's not the sort of greeting you expect from a professor," Jacob joked.

"Professors live in the real world, too! Anyway, never mind the sarcasm, this card came through the door for you a few minutes ago."

The red envelope was larger than usual; it clearly wasn't one from a bargain selection box – it was the sort one would only send to a special friend or loved one. Jacob opened it slowly and carefully; the card had an embossed cartoon bear on the front wearing a 'Santa' hat. Much more important to him was the message on the inside. His hopes were confirmed by the neatly written words that simply read, 'Happy Christmas – love Rachel'. Jacob felt butterflies in his stomach. He would have loved to go down to her house to see her, but it was a family day and he would have felt awkward.

"Who's it from, Jake?" asked the Professor.

"Rachel," replied Jacob nervously.

"Rachel Isaacson?" enquired his uncle.

"Yeah," came the brief reply.

"Well, she's a lovely looking girl," commented the Professor, who decided to question no further, seeing Jacob was acting shyly. "Well, how about, we open those presents…"

Next to the bauble-laden Christmas tree in the lounge was one particularly large box, tagged with Jacob's name. Jacob began stripping off the shiny wrapping paper, revealing cardboard that was labelled with details of the flat screen television inside. "I don't believe it…," he uttered in surprise.

"Yes, I know… I know. I've finally given in. I suppose our minds will be turned to mush by soap operas and reality television, but at least I'll understand what people are talking about at work. No, just kidding – I hope you like it," said Jacob's uncle, giving him an affectionate pat.

They spent the morning opening presents and eating as many chocolates and biscuits as humanly possible. The Professor started reading one of the science books that Jacob had bought him – before deciding that for at least one day, he should give it a rest. Jacob busied himself setting up the television stand and reading the operating instructions. Once everything was ready, they sat back to watch the usual Christmas repeats which, even if to no one else, were new to them.

Christmas dinner was the traditional roast turkey, vegetables and all the trimmings. After washing up, they were back to the sofa in the lounge... and more chocolates. The Professor had been desperate to tell someone the reason why he had been so secretive recently. Now, relaxing on the sofa, he decided to take the risk.

"Jake... you love history. Now, just suppose that you could go to any time in history... which one would you choose?" he questioned as Jacob absentmindedly flicked through the channels.

"It would have to be... yes, it would have to be 1066, before the Battle of Hastings. I would love to go there and warn King Harold to rest his army before taking on the Normans," replied Jacob thoughtfully.

"Yes, they should have won. It was a mistake marching all that way down to the South and fighting another battle – so soon after defeating the Vikings in the North," stated the Professor, steeling himself for what he was going to tell Jacob next...

"You know, Jacob, philosophers and academics talk with great certainty about their understanding of time – as they do about a lot of matters. Actually, you have to appear certain about things if you want funding, and that's fine by me. However, time is something that is hard even to define. Even the 'Greats' have differed on their understanding of it. Time in one location of the universe is not necessarily even the same as in another. I do know though, that all moments in time are equally real and I know that from my own experimentation."

"What experimentation?" asked Jacob, a bit confused, which wasn't unusual when his uncle started getting deep.

"I've travelled to the past Jacob," said the Professor with a low, serious-sounding tone in his voice.

"You're winding me up!" Jacob said as he laughed and leant back into the sofa.

Now the Professor took his science very, and I mean *very,* seriously. Nevertheless, Jacob thought that this had to be a joke and he thought he'd look like a fool if he gave his uncle's statement any credence.

"You can't travel back in time, it's not possible... or maybe in a couple of hundred years they'll find a way," said Jacob, waiting for the smile from the Professor that never arrived.

"I agree it sounds insane, I wouldn't have believed it either if someone else had said it. However, I've found a way to the past or at least it found me. As far as I am aware, we and just one other are the only people on this planet who know about it. I had to tell someone, Jake, this is too big a secret to keep to myself."

Jacob was beginning to feel excited and slightly scared at the same time. "If you're serious why don't you tell Dr. Lennox, or one of the other professors?"

"It's too soon, Jake. The implications are massive and I don't want the military finding out about this – I'm not sure how they would use it. I might just share this information with a few others or maybe just hide the time mechanisms where they won't be found," explained the Professor, looking concerned.

It was dawning on Jacob that this wasn't some sort of extremely late or very early April fool's joke. The thought that his uncle was suffering from some sort of breakdown also went through his mind. After all, the Professor had been working very late in his study every night, in recent weeks.

"Okay, well... how about, you show me these 'mechanisms' after this programme ends?"

"Never mind the television, I'll show you now!" his uncle said, leaping up from his chair and heading for the staircase.

The Professor's study was the size of two large double bedrooms, which in fact it had been until he had had the partition wall removed. The walls were covered with oak panelling, the ceiling a rather dull off-white. As you might expect in the study of a professor, there were hundreds of books of different sizes. They filled shelves that reached from the floor to the ceiling along one wall of the room. Jacob's uncle drew the heavy curtains across the original Victorian sash windows and proceeded to remove a section of books from the end of the middle shelf. Jacob could now see the small door of a safe he never knew existed.

The Professor lifted out an object wrapped up in a piece of worn leather, which he carried to his desk, laying it down with great care. "Here it is," he said. "Actually, I have two of them. I call them 'time mechanisms' for want of a better name. I've tried to date them, but I just get contradictory dates for their age, which make no sense."

The 'time mechanism' was a small, cedar wood box about twelve centimetres in length and width, and about seven centimetres in depth. The top of the box featured an ornate carving of a seven-branched candlestick. The carving was flanked by two rectangular windows on each side, with small brass dials below, that would alter numbers in the windows when turned. The front had twelve more rectangular windows, which also had behind each a number and dials below. From each side of the box protruded a small brass lever that could move either up or down, but not stop in the middle. Below each lever there was a brass button.

"There is a kind of switch on the back of the box, which I believe governs whether the years are AD or BC," commented the Professor as he picked the box up again.

"Where did you get it?" Jacob asked.

"On the island of Antikythera, one of the Greek islands. Some amazing artefacts have been discovered there, like the 'Antikythera Mechanism' – a kind of 2000-year-old analogue computer. However, as I said, it found me rather than the other way round. It was last summer, when I went on that Greek Island break while you were on holiday with the school. A boy of Middle-Eastern appearance came up to me in the main marketplace near my hotel. He then put a box down in front of me containing this device and the other, which is in the safe. I picked it up and he started walking backwards, then turned and ran."

"Who was he?" asked Jacob, his curiosity growing by the minute.

"I have no idea, but he looked scared, which isn't surprising considering what he had been holding. The time mechanisms are easy to use, have few parts... and that is the mysterious thing about them. One would expect them to be full of complex machinery and yet they aren't, just a few cogs and levers etc. You could be forgiven for thinking that they were toys of some kind, albeit beautifully crafted ones," the Professor explained.

Jacob's uncle began turning the dials; the numbers rotating until they were in the order he desired, he then pulled down the levers simultaneously. "Okay Jacob we're all set to go... to the past that is. You can come with me or observe and take notes – what would you like to do?" asked the Professor in a matter of fact sort of way, as if this was just an everyday occurrence.

"Er... I think I'll just watch," replied Jacob feeling uneasy. It was clear that this wasn't some sort of joke, and the whole situation seemed increasingly bizarre.

The Professor left the room with the time mechanism and went downstairs and into the hall. He picked up his car keys from the telephone table and began putting on his sheepskin coat.

"Where are we going?" asked Jacob.

"To see an old tree," his uncle smiled... "a four thousand year-old tree..."

Jacob, not quite sure what to do, opted to go along with this apparent delusion. He hoped that the inevitable failure of attempting time travel might somehow bring the Professor to his senses.

In a funny way, he felt he'd rather be with his uncle on his strange misadventure, than anywhere else on this Christmas Day – even than with Rachel Isaacson. He considered that this was his uncle's hour of need and after all, his uncle had always been there for him. The Professor had brought Jacob up like his own son, ever since his parents' mysterious disappearance. They had gone missing while making a television documentary in Ethiopia. Jacob had only been two years old at the time and was found wandering around the streets of Axum by some market traders.

It was by now three o'clock in the afternoon, the time of the Queen's Christmas speech to the nation, not that they would be listening to that this time. Outside of the house, it was windy and cold, but there wasn't any snow. The few flakes that had greeted him as he had left St. Nicholas' Church the day before having melted away.

The Professor pressed a button on his remote control key fob, setting the automatic, double garage door into motion. The garage door raised up and over, to reveal his pride and joy: a 1965 Bentley S3 Continental 'Flying Spur'. The much cherished car looked resplendent in its Oxford Blue as it set off from Wigglesworth Road, down the even quieter than usual country lanes. Inside, its light grey leather seats contrasted with the dark blue carpet and the wood veneer of the dashboard.

"Why are we going to see an old tree? What's that got to do with time travel?" Jacob asked, wondering what on earth they were doing now.

"It's a four thousand year-old yew tree, at least it's thought to be. Yews are very hard to date, but they are the oldest living trees in Europe," answered his uncle as they reached a roundabout.

"Sure... but why are we going to see it?" asked Jacob, still waiting for a more complete answer.

"What would happen, Jake, if we travelled forward or back in time from our house?"

"I don't know... did you say forward in time!" gasped Jacob, thinking his uncle really was 'away with the fairies'.

"Never mind about the future for now – if we move to another time, we need to arrive in an open space. For example, if we travel from our house we don't know into what space we will appear. We could travel back a thousand years and materialise inside a solid object like a wall in the same place. Therefore, we need to find a safer spot for our departure, such as the old yew tree in Crowhurst. We know there has been nothing in its place or next to it for about four thousand years," explained Jacob's uncle as he parked the 'Flying Spur' by a grass verge in the small village. "Here we are, we could call this place the 'Timeport', you know... instead of the airport, a time..."

"...port – yeah, I get it," said Jacob rolling his eyes, "But, if it doesn't work, don't worry... we'll just go back home and have some turkey sandwiches. Oh, and there's a really good film on later..."

Jacob hoped that his uncle wouldn't be too badly crushed, when this time travel experiment inevitably ended in farce.

Chapter Three

The Old Tree

They crossed the road to St. George's Church and passed through the lychgate into the churchyard. In front of the 12th century church building stood a very old-looking tree. The huge trunk of the yew was almost ten metres in girth. It was so big and hollowed out with age that people could actually walk around inside it and gaze up through the branches above, from within. There was even a door fitted into it, as its hollowed inner had been used as a small room in times past, even once furnished with a table and benches. If a tree could talk, then surely this one would have had a great deal to say. It would not only have spoken of people from different eras, but also of battle – a cannonball from the English civil war had once been found in it.

"Actually, Jacob, I think it would be best if you come with me rather than just observe. We shall stand close to the tree without touching it. Whilst doing so I want you to put one of your hands on my head," said the Professor, holding the time mechanism.

"Do I have to? It's really embarrassing – suppose somebody sees me," said Jacob looking around, just to make sure they really were alone.

"I thought you weren't worried about what other people think of you. Never mind other people, scientific advance never came from following the crowd. Now listen carefully, you need to be in contact with the person holding the Time Mechanism, otherwise you'll be left behind. Now what year do you wish to go to?" asked his uncle with a grin.

"Er... 1066," said Jacob, it being the first year that popped into his mind. "So, how does it work?"

"It has worked, look around you!" laughed the Professor.

Jacob stepped away from the tree, which now was no longer hollow at its base. The wooden support, which had helped prop up one of its larger ageing branches, had gone. The hinged door in the tree was also missing, and the church building, which had been replaced by an earlier flint and stone one, now had a thatched roof rather than tiles.

"No way! I can't believe it... take me back... take me back!" demanded Jacob, his voice growing louder as fear and panic began to overtake him.

In a blur, everything reverted to the way that it had been.

"It's alright, Jake – everything's okay. I thought you wanted to time travel," said the Professor, a bit confused at his nephew's reaction.

"I'm sorry... I just didn't believe it was possible; I thought you were going mad!" said Jacob, shaking like a leaf in the wind.

After the shock to Jacob from the experience, they decided to return home and relax. The Professor built up the fire in the lounge, while his nephew was busy in the kitchen. Jacob made them some turkey and pickle sandwiches and filled a plate with an assortment of finger food and savoury dips. In an attempt to return to normality they sat down to watch one of the Christmas movies while they ate.

The film was gripping. It was the first time that he and his uncle had sat down to watch a whole movie together, apart from a few rare trips to the cinema. Even as engrossed as he was, Jacob found it impossible to prevent his thoughts from wandering back to time travel and its implications. Some doubts also came into his mind as to whether the things he saw were real or just some kind of trick of the mind. As the movie ended and the adverts returned, Jacob pressed the mute button on his remote. "Good film, wasn't it?"

"Yes, it was better than I expected," agreed the Professor.

"I've been thinking… about what happened earlier with the time thing… I want to give it another go. How about we go down to that old tree again – I'm ready now… I was just a bit freaked out by it all," said Jacob, although the thought of it did still give him butterflies in his stomach.

"There's no rush, 'tomorrow's another day', as Scarlet O'Hara would say," his uncle answered, as he leaned back into his armchair, glass of wine in hand, and put his feet upon a foot stool. "In fact, why rush to do anything when you can simply go back in time, whenever you please and do it all again," he said, feeling pretty pleased with himself.

To Jacob it was all pretty overwhelming. He could understand why the Professor needed to share the secret with at least one other person. It was rather scary to possibly be one of only two or three people on the planet – in the universe even – who seemed to have this knowledge. This begged certain questions: Where and how did these time travel devices originate? And who was responsible for their creation?

"The… er… time boxes or 'time mechanisms', I think you called them… they're ancient, aren't they? I mean, no one makes devices out of wood these days, and I've never seen anything like them. So how can someone have made a time travel device years ago, when we can't even do it today?"

"I admit they have the appearance of age, Jacob, but as I said earlier – I can't get any date reading on them at all."

"Maybe they came from the originator of the 'Big Bang', or however the universe really came about," teased Jacob with a smile.

"There is no 'originator' of the kind I think you mean, and real science dismisses that as an option not worth investigating."

With that, the Professor went upstairs to bed, leaving Jacob to think of all the possibilities that lay before him. He wondered how time travel might affect them, would it stop them from ageing? Could they bring things back from the past? What if they altered the past? And other such questions. Most of all he pondered the possibility of going back in time a relatively short way and finding out what happened to his parents.

The Christmas holiday of 2010 was to become a voyage of exploration, not to exotic distant lands but to different times in familiar places. Most people, before travelling, will investigate potential holiday destinations via glossy travel brochures or online. Jacob, however, spent most of Boxing Day morning scouring the Internet for local history. He was busy trying to find exciting events down the centuries, that could be visited a short distance from the Old Tree. Jacob also started looking at web sites featuring Ethiopia, saving them for a later time.

The Old Tree was the almost perfect local departure point. However, there were plenty of other reasonably good alternatives elsewhere. Castles, ruined monasteries, old bridges, public houses and other such historic places around the United Kingdom also offered opportunities for travel. Man-made structures needed to be carefully researched though and carried more risks of collision with other people. Unexpected objects such as carts and outbuildings that were no longer in existence and had never been recorded were also dangers.

The Professor wouldn't let Jacob travel without him, even though he had tried the time mechanisms a number of times without a problem. However, with the university closed for Christmas, it was the ideal time to travel together.

"Jacob, do you fancy going on a little trip?" his uncle called up the stairs.

"How little?" answered Jacob, trying to be heard over the loud volume of the music in his room.

"Two miles and about seventy years, come on, let's go," ordered the Professor as he put on his favourite 'Newbury' brown hat and sheepskin coat.

Jacob wasn't too concerned about where (or when, I should say) they were going. He just wanted to try the experience again. If the experience was real and not just some imagination or hallucination, then perhaps the mystery of his parents' disappearance really could be solved.

The Professor was already waiting outside in the 'Flying Spur' by the time Jacob left the house. Two miles of driving down country lanes took them to the small village of South Godstone. The village was dissected by a main road connecting London and the South Coast. Jacob's uncle parked the Bentley in a lay-by on the main road. From there, they crossed the road into a farmer's field – a safe area for departure, as it had also been just a field in the time they were to visit.

"What happened in South Godstone then?" enquired Jacob, a bit surprised at his uncle's choice of destination. Jacob couldn't remember reading of any major events going on there. South Godstone was a newer village than Godstone itself, having sprung up around an outlying railway station in the 1800s.

"See for yourself, Jake," said the Professor as passing cars and vans were replaced by civilian coaches filled with soldiers.

Weary, very weary looking soldiers were pouring out of the railway station further down the road. They weren't all smart – some wore dirty, dishevelled uniforms, with faces unshaven, and many wounded. Local villagers were walking amongst the throng with trays full of cups of tea and whatever food they could offer. Others stood about, penning notes on scraps of paper. These they gave to the locals, to pass the message on to their loved ones that they were alive.

"What's happening?" Jacob asked, feeling rather conspicuous in his modern clothes.

"They're just back from the beaches of Dunkirk. They're part of an army of over three hundred and thirty thousand who were rescued from the French beaches. They had the sea on one side and an unstoppable, at that point, German army on the other. The Royal Navy and 700 little ships such as fishing boats crossed the channel to get them. The evacuation of the troops was called the 'Miracle of Dunkirk'. If these troops had been captured, we would have lost the war. A lot of these will be going back to France in a few years to help liberate it," stated his uncle.

Jacob felt humbled at the sight before him, wondering how he would have coped if he had lived during that war. He also felt a great admiration for the courage of these people and the way everyone was helping each other. He wanted to shout out, to tell them not to worry – that they would win, but he wasn't sure if that was the right thing to do.

"Do you reckon we should tell them what's going to happen, about the Battle of Britain, Pearl Harbour, Stalingrad and all the turning points of the war? They probably wouldn't believe us at first – but as each event turned out as we said, they'd be really encouraged," said Jacob.

"Best not... but to be honest, I'm not sure myself. In science fiction books they would probably say 'don't change the past because it affects the future' – but then the past and future aren't always as we'd like."

Since Jacob's first trip he'd imagined they would be hopping from one time to another – just like channel surfing on a television or radio. The powerful emotions engendered by what they were witnessing, suddenly made flitting through different times seem disrespectful. As a result, they decided to make no more than one 'time journey' a day, planning the journey in the morning and travelling in the afternoon. Each was recorded meticulously on a computer and they carefully took photos and video footage of the people and places they saw.

The Professor, still unable to understand what made the time mechanisms work, tested them before and after each journey. He tried to discover if some kind of signal might have been emanating from them – but found nothing. Inevitably, the pair made attempts at travelling to the future. However, each time future dates were set, the levers on the sides of the box would lock, denying them access to the future. For the time being, at least.

Following wartime Britain, they explored Tudor England – well, part of it anyway. They visited Hever Castle, childhood home of Anne Boleyn, on a day when the monstrous King Henry VIII was visiting. Jacob wished he could have warned Anne that her future marriage to this man would ultimately lead to her execution. He knew though, that if he had attempted to do so, he would certainly have been arrested.

Jacob also got his wish granted to see properly the fateful events of October 1066. They drove to an area within sight of the battlefield and 'arrived' in time to see the start of the battle between the army of King Harold and the Norman invaders. The brutality of what they witnessed as Harold's heroic Saxons defended Senlac Hill against William's army of mercenaries was too much to bear. They felt ashamed that they were viewing the battle in much the same way the Romans used to watch the unfortunate gladiators in the arena.

As the Professor operated the time mechanism, the noise of death and hell vanished from their ears. The battlefield scene with its thousands of combatants was now gone. Only a scattering of people remained, wandering about whilst trying to imagine what had once gone on. "They're better off not knowing," he said, nodding grimly in the direction of the tourists.

They drove almost in silence for most of the journey home, just breaking the quiet with the occasional small talk. That evening found them back on the sofa in front of the television, which was now almost as dominant in their lives as the time mechanisms. "Tomorrow night, I'm going out with Rachel to the cinema," Jacob mentioned as he reached for another crisp from the table.

"I'll drive you there if you want, but I'd still like to travel tomorrow... I want to show you entertainment – Victorian style!" his uncle said excitedly.

'Victorian style' didn't sound like much fun to Jacob. He had always thought of the Victorians as rather dour and overly serious. Still, he didn't mind – it was his uncle's turn to choose where to go and all he was concerned about was his first date with Rachel. The past couldn't be better than that.

The next morning, after a fried breakfast of egg and sausages, great for the taste buds if not the heart, the Professor brought in a box of clothes from the car. "Choose a suit, Jake," he said as he lay the box on the floor of the kitchen.

"You must be joking!" said Jacob as he searched through the clothes.

Jacob ended up looking very much the Victorian gentleman with silk puff tie, spectacular paisley patterned waistcoat, pinstriped trousers, white shirt with silver buttons and a black wool frock coat.

"You should wear it tonight, Rachel would love it," his uncle said, laughing at his own suggestion. "You're missing one thing though," he added as he went into the cloakroom and brought out a top hat.

"What are you gonna do – pick a rabbit out of it?" mocked Jacob. He felt rather stupid going out of the house dressed like that. Jacob may not have believed in following the crowd, but this was a bit much even for him.

Again they drove to Crowhurst, home of the Old Tree, making sure no one was looking before they got out of the car and went into the churchyard. (Now, it should be said at this point that time brings many changes. Language doesn't stand still, but for the sake of clarity, the dialogue with people from the past has been translated. Although the odd 'thee' and 'thou' has been left to preserve the fragrance of ages past...)

From alongside the Old Tree they again departed from 2010 and this time arrived in the year 1870. Jacob no longer felt embarrassed by what he was wearing and actually felt quite sophisticated as he and the Professor walked back out through the churchyard. The pathway could no longer be seen, it having been coated with a generous blanket of snow. He still didn't know why they were there – the Professor was keeping it secret. There were a few dwellings close to the churchyard, the area around being mostly fields and farm buildings. As they gazed at their surroundings, they heard the clip-clop of horses' hooves in the distance. The sound heralded the convenient approach of a carriage, drawn by two black horses.

Jacob's uncle waved his hand in the air and the driver slowed the horses down to a halt. "Can you take us to the railway station, my good man?" The driver, a man in his fifties wearing a heavy coat, accepted the request – and after paying their fare, they were off down the country lanes.

"Hark at you... saying 'my good man'," Jacob whispered, with a shake of the head.

From horse and coach to steam train, they made their journey to London. The tracks took them past long rows of terraced houses with smoke billowing from their chimneys.

They also travelled through fields, some of which have been replaced today with sprawling housing estates. The destination was St. James's Hall, the then hub of the London music scene.

Once they had reached Piccadilly Circus station, they made the short walk to the entrance of the Hall in Regent Street. As they arrived at the front of the queue, Jacob was surprised to see the Professor produce two rather crumpled tickets, which had completely yellowed with age. "Where did you get those? Have you been here before?"

"No, I bought them at an auction on the Internet. They were sold as memorabilia – they were never used."

"And the money?"

"My old coin collection," his uncle answered.

The smartly dressed woman in the ticket office looked at the tickets curiously for a few seconds before allowing them through. They followed the crowds up one of the ornate wooden staircases into the great hall, which was to accommodate the audience of over two thousand people who were rapidly filling the seats.

An orchestra was playing some music by Handel. Jacob, who was now expecting an evening of classical music, wished he had sneaked in his portable music player.

"How long is this going on for?" asked Jacob, getting worried.

"Just sit back and enjoy it, Jake."

The gas lighting was turned off and a hush fell upon the audience. The huge curtains hiding the stage were pulled back to reveal a solitary, yet somehow familiar figure.

"The Carol," announced the performer as every eye in the hall was fixed upon him. Absolute silence, but for this man. He continued, "...Marley was dead to begin with. There is no doubt whatever about that. The register of his burial was signed by the clergyman, the clerk, the undertaker, and the chief mourner. Scrooge signed it..." The changes in the tone of his voice brought each character to life, energy that brought pictures to the mind as clear as in any film.

"Charles Dickens reading the Christmas Carol... are you impressed, Jake?"

He was.

His uncle nudged him and whispered: "His last ever performance..."

Chapter Four

Dark Clouds Looming

Rachel was no Charles Dickens, and Jacob was quite glad about that. Charles may have been a literary colossus and seeing him hold an audience spellbound just by reading was amazing – but a night out with Rachel was in a totally different sphere.

She was of both Syrian and U.S. descent. Her father was an American businessman from Texas and her mother a former reporter for a Syrian newspaper. She was blessed with beauty, brains and, most of all, a good heart. No one's perfect, but Rachel was to Jacob.

Rachel spent a lot of time studying. She was aware that she had a good chance of getting a place at a prestigious university like Oxford or Cambridge, as her older sister had. Rachel had been bullied at school for a time for being too 'bookish', but those days were now behind her. She had her sights firmly set on eventually becoming a cosmologist. She had been fascinated with space and with understanding the universe from a young age. Her family had lived near Houston in Texas, where she was born. They had visited the Space Center there a number of times. Moving to a small English village when she was twelve had been quite a change, but she had grown to love it. She did miss the hot climate, but the countryside was beautiful and London with its attractions was a fairly short train journey away.

Jacob had been keen on Rachel for some time and was

feeling a bit nervous as he prepared for their evening out. He made sure he was dressed in his best clothes. He even used a bit of his uncle's most expensive after-shave, just to add a touch of sophistication. Everything had to be just right, or so he thought.

"I've wanted to do this for so long," said Jacob as they started the three-mile journey to the town of Oxted. Rachel had recently passed her driving test and was driving them there in the hatchback she borrowed from her mother.

"What, go to the cinema?"

"No, to go out with you."

"Ah, that's really nice, Jake – I'm glad to… you're more mature than most of the guys I know. Even though some of them are older than you, they mostly just want to get smashed out of their heads. They're never serious."

Jacob thought he had better behave pretty seriously on hearing that – but then again, he didn't want to come across as boring either. Having found a place to park, they walked together a short way, down the hill to the cinema. In keeping with his recent activities, the building presented him with both the technology of today as well as the image of the past. The frontage was Tudor, mock rather than original, and the attractive interior was timbered in like manner. It was a theatre that had showcased Hollywood's finest for about eighty years and one of the last, single-screen cinemas.

Once inside, they bought tickets for a romantic comedy film. Jacob would rather have seen something with a few explosions and a car chase, but perhaps this wasn't the night for that. Next was the visit to the kiosk to stock up on the obligatory popcorn, before ascending the red carpeted stairs to the auditorium where they found their seats. Halfway through the film, he snaked an arm around Rachel's shoulders, who, to his great relief, snuggled up against him in response. Jacob didn't pay much attention to the rest of the light drama on the screen. He just sat there in the joy of knowing that Rachel Isaacson was now his girlfriend.

Winter bade farewell and spring arrived as Jacob and Rachel's relationship blossomed. Often Mr and Mrs Isaacson would invite Jacob over for dinner, introducing him to traditional Middle-Eastern cuisine. Jacob and Rachel were far from being typical teenagers, something they had in common. They both despised the way people were pressured into conforming to others' expectations – in what to wear, to listen to and what to like in general. Together, they felt the freedom to do what they wanted to do – and to think for themselves. Life for Jacob now seemed almost perfect... but nothing remains that way forever – and this was to be no exception.

With Jacob spending more time with Rachel or studying, the Professor again found himself making many of the time journeys alone. He had got absolutely nowhere in trying to understand how the time mechanisms worked; the fact was that they should not have been working at all. All their components appeared to do was to merely change the numbers that appeared in the tiny windows on the exterior. It was a mystery and it was beginning to disturb him. If he couldn't understand how they worked, that made them unpredictable to a degree... and this lack of predictability left an element of danger.

However, as the number of journeys increased, the time mechanisms themselves became much less of an object of study and more a method of time tourism – without real purpose. The detailed analysis that marked the earlier journeys was replaced with a few scribbled notes on a pad, just mentioning the destinations and dates. The lack of progress he had made was beginning to make him reconsider whether he should bring others in to assist with their secret discovery. However, this was still balanced by the dangers as to what might happen if knowledge of the time mechanisms became widespread.

The Professor considered that everything had a natural explanation. Even if he couldn't understand the time mechanisms' abilities – a natural explanation would have to be found. At least for now, the responsibility for finding one would remain with him, even if he didn't yet know where to look. Supernatural explanations were, to him, unscientific and not to be considered. The origin and existence of life and all matter were merely part of a natural process, with no need to look to the divine to provide an answer. He viewed such concepts as being most unwelcome and worthy of contempt.

Frustrations with the mystery of the time mechanisms didn't, however, take away the sheer excitement of the experience of time travel. He may not have understood their abilities or purpose – but then, to the Professor, life had no particular purpose anyway. You lived, you died, and that was it… although it was right and good to help the next generation keep the human species going.

As the months of 2011 went by, the Professor explored time, whilst Rachel was busy studying for the exams that would mould her future. She had been studying maths, physics, and history at A level. Jacob knew she would pass with flying colours and was more concerned about being apart from her when she was at university. Jacob had, so far, somehow managed to keep the time mechanisms secret from Rachel. However, it was becoming increasingly hard to do so. With her birthday not far away, he wished he could take her on a 'date' she would never forget.

One summer afternoon, after Rachel's exams had finished, they were on one of their walks through the countryside – something they loved to do. The particular route they were on took them towards the village of Crowhurst, where the 'Old Tree' had stood for so many centuries. Thinking of his and the Professor's favourite departure point up ahead, he dared to hint at his secret: "Rachel, what would you say, if I told you that time travel is possible?"

"I'd say you're nuts, Jake. Why – does Professor Ketterley believe it?"

"Yes, he does and he knows someone who has done it, but don't say anything... it's really important that it remains a secret."

"Come on Jake, whoever it was who said they time travelled must be lying... or on something. It would be fun if it was true though," said Rachel. "Perhaps your uncle was winding you up."

"He wouldn't joke about something like that." Jacob stopped walking and pointed at a gap between some bushes. "Anyway, have you ever seen that really old yew tree in the churchyard over there?"

They made their way across a field where some cows were grazing. Climbing over the stile at the far end, they found their way into the back of the churchyard.

"This is it – amazing, isn't it?" Jacob said as he led them to the front of the church building where the ancient tree stood.

"Well, as old trees go, I suppose," Rachel answered with a smile, "it is pretty unusual."

The hollow area of the trunk of the tree made Jacob wonder how it was still alive. Yet the mass of leaves above bore testimony to the fact that it would be around for a while longer yet.

"Look at that little door!" Rachel exclaimed. "It's like something out of an Enid Blyton book." Memories of the 'Faraway Tree' stories were rekindled by the small locked door that had been set into the trunk long ago.

"Yeah, there was a little room in there once," said Jacob as they went inside the hollowed out part of the tree.

"It's a bit weird in a way, isn't it? I mean, to think that this tree has been alive while so many people passing by it have

come and gone," Rachel said as she gazed upwards at the expanse of branches.

Jacob was desperate to tell Rachel of his time travels, but managed to stop himself. Although he did try again at opening her up to the possibilities.

"How can you dismiss time travel but go to church and believe in the existence of God?" he asked bluntly.

"Well, I think there are many good reasons to believe. Maybe a lot of people would rather he didn't exist," replied Rachel, a bit surprised by Jacob's question.

"No, we're just here because of the 'Big Bang' and evolution, that's all. It's a scientific fact," Jacob stated.

"We exist because we exist, there is no reason or purpose to it."

"Well, evolution doesn't disprove the existence of God. Some people even believe that the scientific evidence is more in favour of some kind of design," she disagreed.

"That's just pseudo-science. Appearance of design doesn't mean there is design, everything is just here by a random process," said Jacob, regretting now that he had stopped studying science. Which he had – just to be different from his uncle.

"Jake, people say that the world appears designed but it isn't really – it's just appearance. I reckon that if something looks like a duck, waddles like a duck, quacks like a duck… then it is probably a duck."

"Well anyway, what if you could travel through time?" Jacob persisted, realising that he'd strayed too far from his subject.

"It would be great fun, Jake, but why do you keep going on about it? It's just science fiction."

Jacob knew it would be a mistake to keep pushing the issue. Even if he could convince Rachel of the possibilities of time travel, he had promised the Professor that he wouldn't tell anyone about the time mechanisms. Besides, both time mechanisms were kept in the safe, so he couldn't take Rachel on a journey without his uncle's permission – and obtaining it seemed unlikely.

"I love you, Rach – sorry for having a go at what you believe. The idea of time travel is just interesting, that's all."

They deliberately kept away from any serious discussions as they made the journey home. They walked arm in arm most of the way, chatting and making jokes. Jacob considered that this had been the best year of his life so far and wished that this summer could last forever. Seasons of life can change more quickly than seasons of time – and this time of tranquillity was about to reach its end.

Back in Wigglesworth Road, the Professor was at his desk, as he had a number of lectures to prepare. He was determined to get them done and out of the way before his next time journey. The journeys themselves had become almost addictive and were beginning to get in the way of his work – nothing had ever done that before. One of the time mechanisms was sitting on his desk; he found it somehow comforting having it near and at times would pause from his work just to look at it. When he was satisfied that he'd put in a good shift and was due a 'tea break', he leaned back into his chair and found that he could barely see the mechanism, which had become a blur. The Professor rubbed his eyes and turned his head away to find everything else in the room was in perfect focus. Again, he looked toward the time mechanism, which remained a distorted blur of shape and colour. Feeling rather dizzy as he gazed at it, he stretched out his hand to touch it...

Professor Ketterley opened his eyes as he lay in the bushes; his grazed left leg hooked over a forked branch. He was desperately gasping for air and felt like he had been knocked down by a heavyweight boxer. He remained still while he recovered before disentangling his limbs and slowly getting to his feet. He remembered touching the blurring box. He realised that he had travelled from his upstairs study and fallen from that height. Concerns about bruising and scratches were soon replaced with panic, when he discovered that the time mechanism was missing.

In the coolness of the morning, he fell to his knees and scrambled around the undergrowth. He desperately tried to find the little box, which was his only transport home. His fear increased as doubts arose as to whether the mechanism was even there at all. Suddenly, he felt a burning pain in his side, knocking the air out of his lungs again – but this time from a hefty kick that sent him rolling across the ground.

"Looking for something?" came the growl of the huge man who had crept up on his blind side. His attacker had greying hair down to his shoulders and a knitted 'Monmouth' hat on his head; his skin ravaged from years at sea and excessive drinking. He was wearing a doublet, deep blue velvet breeches and waistcoat, his boots that had dealt the blow came up to his thighs. This fearsome individual stood over poor Professor Ketterley, twisting his large gold hooped earring with one hand. More worryingly, his other hand rested on a dagger in his wide leather belt – which also held three pistols.

The Professor raised his hands in the air to make it absolutely clear that he was no threat. "I'm unarmed, I mean you no harm," he said, his heart beating rapidly.

The old pirate laughed and drew his dagger from its holder, "Thou mean'st no harm eh? Well I do. Now, I know not who thou art and I care even less. Another matter be that little box thou wast carrying... worth good money. Of that I be sure."

Jacob's uncle felt relieved that this thug knew of the time mechanism's whereabouts and his mind raced, thinking of a way of escape. "Do you have the treasure?" he asked, growing in confidence as an idea developed in his mind.

"Treasure?"

"Promise to spare my life and it's yours."

"Trenchie don't do deals!" said the pirate as he raised the dagger to the Professor's throat. "Treasure... thou think'st me a fool?"

The Professor was left with a terrible choice: lose his life or lose his only way home. "The box... it contains fine jewels and gold, small but worth a lot of money. See for yourself – just open it. On each side of the box is a lever, pull them downwards and then press the buttons below the levers simultaneously."

"Ugh?" grunted 'Trenchie'.

"Press them at the same time."

The pirate took the time mechanism from inside his doublet and stepped back from the Professor, who was still on the ground. He quickly put the dagger back into its holder, and pulled the levers. Impatient to see the 'treasure', he pressed the buttons...

Professor Ketterley felt stranded, like an astronaut lost in space with no one to help. He didn't know where he was – or perhaps it would be better to say, 'when he was'. He hadn't reset the dates on the Mechanism since his last return journey to 2011... so how could he be some centuries in the past? And why had the mechanism appeared as a blur when he was back in the study? More pressing, however, was the immediate situation – he needed to find a roof over his head, food, and water; everything else would have to wait.

Chapter Five

A Country Garden

Jacob finished his cup of tea around at the Isaacsons' house and, after saying goodbye, made the short walk to his home. It had been over two weeks since Jacob's last time journey and he was missing the thrill that 'travelling' gave. Observing people and places of the past never ceased to lose its attraction for Jacob. The scary part was always the return journey – what would happen if the Time Mechanism stopped working or was somehow lost? While travelling together, he and his uncle always took both devices with them. When the Professor travelled alone, he would leave Jacob a note detailing 'when' he was going to and the safe unlocked.

Time travel had been a bit like a trip to the zoo or maybe more like an African safari, just observing from a safe distance. Jacob didn't care that much about how the time mechanisms worked, although the mysterious way they came into their possession intrigued him. He wondered why the boy who brought them to his uncle seemed so afraid. Whatever the reason and however it all worked, he was confident his uncle would get to the bottom of it.

Jacob thought that the future looked really bright for him and his uncle. Perhaps they would be able to sell the time mechanisms for millions of pounds, or sell one and secretly keep the other. Surely, Jacob considered, his uncle was a certainty for a Nobel Prize of some sort – but then again, he hadn't actually invented them, and if they fell into the wrong hands…

"Hi, I'm back!" he called as he took off his trainers, leaving them on the door mat. No answer came and so he made his way up the staircase and on into the study. The safe was closed, so he assumed his uncle was in the garden, probably reading a selection of newspapers.

From the partially opened sash window Jacob had a good view of the back garden. They were no gardeners, but the Professor regularly employed someone to take care of it. Close to the patio were beds with a mix of flowers and small shrubs, with the foxgloves, geraniums and sweet peas adding warmth and colour as they bloomed. Beyond the flowerbeds was a lawn approximately forty metres in length, ending where it met a dense privet hedge. The thick wall of hedge was only broken by a gap in the middle, leading to an area of woodland.

Jacob thought he saw the Professor as he looked toward the gap in the hedge and returned down the staircase. He put his trainers back on and walked across the lawn and through the gap in the hedge, the heat of the summer sun beginning to fade.

"Halt just there, boy, or die!" came a low voice from behind Jacob as he entered the woodland.

A shiver ran through Jacob's body as he saw the bewildering pirate through the corner of his eye, taking aim with a pistol.

"Now tell me, boy, is death here?"

If it was, a pistol wouldn't have been much use, but Jacob wasn't about to say that.

"Don't be afraid… this isn't hell. This is Godstone… in 2011."

The pirate was confused, but not scared – only death scared him, though he wouldn't admit it. He had supposed death to be a 'Grim Reaper' type figure and, despite having introduced many to him, wasn't so keen on making that acquaintance himself. It was now obvious to the 17th century pirate that something amazing had taken place – and not necessarily a bad thing, either. However, there was something else he would need to know, "Are there any of the King's men nearby?"

"Er… no, and actually we have a Queen now… and she's alright – she doesn't have anyone killed. So please, can you put the gun down now?"

The old pirate lowered his pistol, "Do as I say, boy, or meet death… now get me strong liquor and some food."

Jacob was scared but tried to remain calm, hoping for a way out of the situation. He led the way back into the house, his heart pounding. "Better find some rum," he muttered, thinking of what the stereotypical pirate might drink.

The Professor's drink cabinet was pretty full of everything except rum, but did find a bottle of whisky with a glass. His 'guest' wasn't interested in using the glass, but simply poured great swigs of the alcohol down his throat. A drunk pirate would be easy to outwit, or so Jacob thought. Years of hard drinking while away at sea – and on land – had ravaged the old sailor's insides. However, he was so used to it that it took a large quantity to get him really drunk.

"There's plenty more, help yourself," said Jacob.

"Wilt thou not be drinking with me, boy?"

"No, no… I'm really not that thirsty, but thanks for offering."

"Drink!" ordered the pirate.

Jacob had drunk wine on certain occasions, usually with a nice meal, but that was about it. With the intruder glaring at him, he took some big gulps from the bottle. His mind soon became fogged up by the intoxicating liquid. He tried to combat its effects, wanting to be in full control of his senses.

"So this is the future, eh… art thou rich? Must be, look at

this finery and what are those glasses for?" the pirate asked as he pointed to the spotlights in the ceiling.

"Lights, don't be afraid, I'll put them on."

"I've killed a hundred men or more, travelled the oceans, been hunted by the King's men, I be afeared of nothing." The old pirate showed no obvious surprise as he saw electricity at work for the first time when Jacob flicked the switch. "Beautiful those lights, very bright – take one out and give it me."

Jacob stood on a stool feeling a bit dizzy with the whisky and removed a bulb. "Here you are, you can keep it."

"Make it work!"

"I can't, it needs to be connected to the lighting circuit."

"Make it work… !" shouted the pirate, reaching for his dagger.

A ring from the doorbell interrupted the difficult situation. "What is that?" whispered the unwelcome guest.

"Somebody is at the door."

"Soldiers perhaps? … Come on boy, with all thy riches I wager you have got some roughs to look out for thee." The intruder moved behind Jacob and prodded him towards the oak front door.

Jacob could just make out Rachel's face through the small square of frosted glass in the door. He was glad to see her, but also worried at the thought of his girlfriend being in danger.

"It's my girlfriend – if we ignore the bell, she'll go away."

"Can she cook?"

"Cook?"

"Open the door and keep thy mouth shut."

Jacob had no choice. As the door opened, the pirate's right hand stretched across Rachel's mouth, and he roughly pulled her inside with his left. Using a foot, he slammed the door shut.

"What be an islander girl doing around these parts?" said the villain, surprised at seeing the olive skinned Rachel in Godstone. "Now hear me, girl, I am about to take my hand

from thy mouth but shout not, nor scream, nor try to run...
I have three loaded pistols and I like to use them."

"It's okay, Rach – he's a pirate from the past... I tried to tell
you about time travel. Don't worry, it's going to be alright."
Jacob's words made absolutely no sense to Rachel.

Rachel tried to gather herself together, weighing up the
situation in her mind. "Yes, of course, you're a pirate..." her
voice trembled, "I'd love to hear about your adventures
on the high seas, it must be so exciting. But first, perhaps
I should call your ship and let them know where you are..."
she said as she scanned around, looking for a telephone with
which to call the police.

"Rach, he really *is* a pirate! Let's just do as he says."

"Now wench, fetch me some supper, you two are gonna
help me get along nicely in three thousand and eleven,"
ordered the pirate, still trying to get used to his new but
appealing surroundings.

"Two thousand and eleven actually," Rachel said boldly.

"Don't wind him up!" warned Jacob.

Rachel was none too happy about being called a wench
and being treated like a servant, but she was more scared than
she let on. With the strangely dressed man being armed, she
knew she had to play along with what he said.

Alone in the kitchen, escape would have been easy.
She wouldn't even contemplate it though, as Trenchie had
threatened to shoot Jacob if she ran away. As much as Jacob's
claim that the intruder was from the past seemed ridiculous,
she couldn't help wondering where he had acquired such
authentic looking clothing. Even his accent was different
to any English accent she had ever heard. Rachel managed
to find a couple of fish pies in the freezer. "He's bound to
like those," she muttered as she began defrosting them in the
microwave oven.

Meanwhile, Jacob had been ordered to give a guided tour

of the house. The pirate enquired about the use of every gadget from the pencil sharpener to the laptop. To Jacob's surprise, the stranger, though in awe of the technology, showed no signs of concern at all – neither of being in such a strange environment, nor of being hundreds of years from his own time. "It is most surely wonderful, boy, wonderful," the villain enthused as Jacob introduced him to 21st century gadgetry.

"Sir," said Jacob.

"Thou canst call me Trenchie. Be a good help and I will count thee as one of my mates."

"Er, thanks... Trenchie. Can you tell me how you got here?" asked Jacob, knowing that the fate of his uncle was linked to this man.

"I was hunting rabbit in the woods when I saw something fall from up high into the bushes up ahead a bit, so I ran towards it. When I got there, I saw a stranger dressed in a manner most unusual, just lying still like he was dead. I thought he might be a gent and so I searched him for money; there was none but I did find this nearby." Trenchie took out the Time Mechanism from inside his doublet, carefully making sure he didn't touch any of the wheels, buttons, or levers.

"The man, are you sure he was dead?"

"Dead, he was not. He arose after a time – until I dealt him a kick and knocked him back down again," laughed the pirate.

Jacob felt really angry inside, but managed to keep control of his feelings. "Was it this man?" he asked, holding up a photograph of the Professor.

"Aye... who is he?"

"My uncle, and this is his house."

"Hmm... well he is alive or at least he was when I left him, but lied to me he did... told me there was treasure in this little box, or maybe he was not lying in a way."

"The food is ready," came Rachel's worried voice from

downstairs. She felt very relieved as the unharmed figure of Jacob appeared at the top of the staircase.

They sat down at the dining room table; Trenchie feeling as important as a ship's captain, while Jacob and Rachel busied themselves serving him his meal and a cocktail of drinks.

"Are you John Trenchman?" asked Jacob as the old pirate raised his glass to his lips yet again.

Trenchie's was so shocked by Jacob's question that he dropped his glass of whisky onto the table, unbroken but soaking the table cloth. "How knowest thou that? That cannot be, we're from different times. "

"Yes, but you're history to us and people have written about you. You were one of the pirates who looted Puerto Bello, Panama in 1668. I've read all about it, there were nine or ten warships with about five hundred men under the leadership of Captain Henry Morgan. You attacked and pillaged the place for a fortnight... until the Spanish paid a ransom for you all to leave. Besides who else could you be, how many other pirates have been in Godstone?"

"Pirates to some, privateers to others... we were doing King Charlie a favour... giving the Spanish a hard time. We let 'em have it; we wrecked the place and drank it dry of rum. But like I say we did the King a favour; Morgan even got knighted and I made me enough money to retire from the sea. So, Trenchie's been remembered, bit like Robin Hood eh?"

"Well, not exactly," remarked Jacob.

"Jake, he's not a pirate. This Trenchman guy has been dead for centuries, he's buried in the churchyard," said Rachel.

She then turned her face towards Trenchie and spoke calmly to him, "Look, let us sort this thing out together, there's no need to get the police involved. Just let me make a phone call to some people who can help you – but you must put your weapons away or you'll be in trouble."

"What's she on about?" said Trenchie, with a shake of the head.

"Rachel doesn't believe in time travel... I didn't believe my uncle when he told me about it either, I thought he was nuts. But Rachel's right, we do have to do something about all this. You can't live in 2011 without our help. It's a totally different world to the one you've come from and we need your help to get my uncle back.'

"I don't do deals, boy, unless they be on my terms, so what be in it for me?"

"Well, how about this... you find my uncle and bring him back. Then we'll get you your own house with lights that go on and off, taps that flow with hot and cold water, and a box that makes music and..."

"Nay boy, I won't just have that. I will have this very house and everything in it and thou wilt bring me all the food and liquor I desire. But I give thee my word, that thou and thine uncle can lodge here and be my servants."

"Okay, yes – I agree," said Jacob, although he intended to leave Trenchie behind as soon as he found his uncle.

"Words don't mean nothing to me boy – I'll make sure thou keep'st thy word," Trenchie said as he tapped his dagger on the table.

"Yes, alright – now, what was the date when you came across my uncle?"

"It was the summer of 1687, not sure of the date exactly... it was a few days after my old mate Collie had been arrested and taken away by the King's men. He was one of my gang, arrested for fighting he was. The rum always made him see the red mist, I was planning his rescue..."

"Can you put the box on the table and turn the wheels, until you have zeros in all the windows on the front, apart from the last four – in those put 1687," interrupted Jacob.

Trenchie took the time mechanism from his doublet and performed the task as requested. As he turned the wheels, the numbers began to blur. He rubbed his eyes and as he had a second look, the whole of the box faded into a blur and then returned to perfect clarity... only to become a blur once again. "What's it doing?" he asked.

Jacob got up from his chair and leaned over the time mechanism, "I don't know... it's never done that before. Trenchie what was the month when you were back in 1687?"

"July."

Jacob moved his hand towards the time mechanism, only to be stopped by the firm grip of Trenchie's hand on his wrist. "That be my box, boy. I would not have thee disappearing with it," the pirate said, fixing him with a cold stare.

"I wouldn't go without you. I said I needed your help, didn't I?" Jacob replied angrily. "My uncle and I travelled together a lot, all you have to do is be in contact with another person and they will go with you, or we could take the other one from the safe..."

"Other one? And what else be in the safe?" Trenchie asked as he reached towards the box...

Rachel was suddenly all alone. Jacob and the pirate had vanished with the blurring box before they even entered the correct month, let alone the day.

She didn't know what to think or do, but remained frozen for a time. Rachel had thought that Jacob was playing some sort of mind game with the intruder, perhaps trying to lull him into a false sense of security by going along with his delusions.

As the sense of shock subsided, Rachel began to explore her options. Perhaps, she could get the police involved – but what would they do? They would surely never believe her story. If they found the other time travel device, what would happen? She worried most of all that the police might pass it on to some mysterious agency. If that happened, there would be no way to ever get to Jacob or his uncle.

Rachel got up from her chair and ran through the house from room to room in panic, trying to find the safe Jacob had mentioned. She didn't know what she would do if she found it, but she needed to know where it was, as it was the only way of finding him.

It was getting late, her parents would be expecting her back at their house, and her panicked searching was achieving nothing. Not wanting to arouse suspicion she decided to come back the next day and renew the search. Rachel took Jacob's door key, which was lying on the sofa and left, making sure that every door and window was locked. Number 87, Wigglesworth Road had now taken on an enormous importance to Rachel. Its security meant that the other box was safe – and while that was the case, hope remained.

"Hi, Rach, you had a good day?" asked Mr Isaacson as his daughter entered the lounge.

"Yes, it was nice, Dad. I went for a lovely walk with Jake down to Crowhurst, saw that old tree that's supposed to be thousands of years old. Then we had a meal at Professor Ketterley's house… it's been an *interesting* day."

She said goodnight, giving her dad a big hug before going up the stairs to her bedroom. Rachel was feeling emotional, but she didn't want to show it. She was determined to avoid possibly endangering her family by getting them involved. That was particularly hard for her, as she had always shared her problems as well as all her joys with them. Rightly or wrongly, she decided that this was something she would have to get through without their help.

Alone in her room, Rachel fell on her knees and began to pray. She felt nothing – nothing to comfort her immediately, but later that night when she lay down to sleep, a sense of assurance came to her and with it a knowledge, that all was not lost.

Chapter Six

Wrong Number

Rachel was surprised to see daylight through the net curtains of her bedroom window. She would never have expected to have had an unbroken night's sleep after the traumatic events of the previous day. Her motto was 'Don't worry about tomorrow's troubles, today's troubles are enough for today', but she didn't always find it that easy to live out.

Well, tomorrow was now today. She ran through her mind what had happened and what she needed to do – or at least thought she had to do. Rachel hadn't travelled through time – and although something had happened to Jacob and the intruder, she couldn't be sure what. In theory, her task was just a matter of locating the other time travel box, copying what they had done and then finding Jacob. Trying to understand what had happened wasn't a priority.

Once she was dressed and had had breakfast, Rachel went about filling her backpack with items that might be useful in this other place or, more accurately, time that she was intending to go to. Food, drinks, matches, a Swiss army knife she'd used for camping, a battery torch and her mobile phone (well, who was to say it wouldn't work 'then') among other things. Filling the backpack made Rachel feel that she was getting on top of the situation, rather than the other way round. Her mindset was now becoming increasingly optimistic.

Thinking back to the previous evening, Rachel remembered how surprised she had been that Jacob had so much knowledge of 'Trenchie' – or Trenchman, as his full surname was. She was aware that a pirate had been buried in the churchyard. She had even seen his gravestone, but she knew little more about him than his name. Guessing that Jacob had probably found out about him on some web site, she went into her parents' spare bedroom, which was used as an office, and sat down at their computer. Once the machine had started up and she had logged on, she began searching on the Internet.

After a short time, she found a link to a local history site that detailed the life of the pirate who had died far inland, in the village of Godstone. Rachel found it quite creepy – reading about the life and death of a man she had seen only the night before. She felt as if she was taking part in some gothic ghost story, having encountered this strange intimidating character while his bones lay long buried in the churchyard.

The web page described how the pirate, John Edward Trenchman 'retired' from his career at sea and in his later years became the leader of a band of smugglers. Trenchman and his gang would make regular trips from the south coast of England as far inland as Croydon. They would always vary the route in order to avoid detection by 'the King's men', as Trenchman liked to call them. Teams of heavy horses were used to pull the wagons carrying the profitable cargo. Trenchman's connections in the world of piracy would have helped him in making deals with captains of ships in order to acquire the elicit goods.

On his last fateful trip from the coast, he was unaware that he had been betrayed by a friend. This 'friend' had told the authorities which route they were planning to take and when the journey was to be made. The betrayer, a member of the gang, had himself been arrested previously on another matter, but was released in exchange for revealing the crucial information.

The pirate-turned-smuggler and his gang rode up Tilburstow Hill, to the south of Godstone, and were caught entirely by surprise. As they entered a clearing in the woodland, a volley of shots rained down upon them. Chaos ensued; a few of the gang were killed instantly. Trenchman's horse was hit and felled – but he himself was unhurt. The old pirate crouched behind its prone body and returned fire. The first 'Battle of Tilburstow Hill' was short but fierce. The soldiers had surrounded the gang and were well-positioned behind trees – making them difficult to hit in the near darkness.

The smugglers were an easy target in the clearing. Sensing the hopelessness of the situation, Trenchman emerged from behind his horse and with a loud bellow urged his doomed comrades to charge at their enemy, hoping to break through their lines and escape. There were only six men including Trenchman who managed to reach the edge of the clearing and engage the soldiers; the rest were already dead or dying. Most of the six had suffered some wounding, yet they all launched themselves ferociously at their foes. Trenchman was the only one to penetrate the cordon of soldiers, killing two by pistol shot and blade – but at the price of incurring serious wounds to himself.

As balls of lead thudded into the trees and earth around him, Trenchman took cover, trying to see if any of his friends had made it through. Cracks of musket fire continued for a couple of minutes and then ceased, with only the noise of the soldiers shouting to each other to take their place. With all his men now dead, the pirate made his escape through the woods carrying the wounds that would mean his end. Trenchman had fought his last battle. He did, however, manage to get to an inn, the 'Fox and Hounds', where he had some friends. There he was looked after, but later died from his injuries.

Curiously, there was also a legend that the old pirate was buried in an unmarked grave and due to that, a series of mysterious and frightening events occurred. Consequently, he was given a full 'Christian service' and the strange events ceased. One of the unusual claims had been that of a couple of gravediggers, who were chased by a figure in seafarer's clothing after the pirate's burial.

Clicking on to the next page, Rachel discovered more details of the betrayal. A chill went down her spine as she read that Trenchman's betrayer was a man named Richard Collins. She remembered that the intruder had mentioned a friend called 'Collie' the night before. Her realisation that Jacob could be in even greater danger increased when she read that the battle at Tilburstow Hill happened in 1687... the same year that Jacob had appeared to go to.

Rachel left her house with her backpack swung loosely over one shoulder and hurriedly made the short walk to number 87. It felt quite strange entering the house alone and she felt a little scared, as if the pirate might suddenly appear from one of the doorways brandishing some weapon. Putting the backpack down in the hallway, she began again her search for the little box that held the key to Jacob's whereabouts. Not knowing where the safe was located, she decided to search every inch of every room methodically until she found it.

Every room meant just that, and Rachel started by emptying out the cupboard beneath the staircase. It was full of the usual household objects: vacuum cleaner, ironing board and so on, as well as computer parts, which were perhaps more peculiar to this household. The safe, however, was not to be found there – and soon she had searched the entire ground floor as thoroughly as was humanly possible.

Once upstairs, Rachel began by searching the study. In a grey filing cabinet near the Professor's desk, she found, among other things, a pile of photographs of both Jacob and his uncle, wearing various period outfits in locations seemingly back in time. She recognised Hever Castle on a couple of them, with bearded yeomen guarding the front of the drawbridge, where it straddled the moat, and certainly no sign of a tourist.

The next photograph showed the pair outside the ancient landmark of Westminster Abbey in London. The difference being that it was still in the building process, with wooden scaffolding in view. The rest of the photographs followed in a similar vein, some of the locations being more recognisable than others. They were fascinating in themselves, but Rachel didn't want to spend time on anything other than the search.

Having put the photographs back, Rachel continued to search the study, but to no avail, and moved on into the other rooms. Beginning to feel frustrated, she tried looking in the garage, even inside the 'Flying Spur' and then the sheds. Returning into the kitchen, she slumped down and sat on the floor, her back against the wall. "There probably isn't another one of those time box things. Jacob must have been trying to play some sort of trick on Trenchman," she muttered to herself, her head in her hands.

Rachel remained there for a few minutes before hauling herself back up onto her feet. With her hopes diminished but not extinguished, she locked the doors and walked back to her house.

"Hi, love," came her mother's voice from the kitchen. "Have you just been to Jake's?"

"Yes."

"I've got a letter for the Professor that was delivered here by mistake. It's a waste of time, banks writing to him – he doesn't believe in them… he probably keeps his money stashed under the mattress! Anyway, can you give it to him the next time you're around there?"

Rachel took the letter and went upstairs to her bedroom. It was probably just another letter from a bank trawling for custom, but it made her think. "If he doesn't like to keep his money in the banks, then he's bound to store some cash somewhere... in a safe, he must have a safe!" she said out loud.

"Talking to yourself, Rach?" queried Mrs Isaacson as her daughter came back downstairs.

"I know, it's the first sign of madness. I'll see you later, I'm just going to pop back to Jake's house."

She was soon back inside number 87 and again rushing from room to room in her quest. This time she removed every picture from its hook and looked behind every curtain to try to find the safe, but again only to draw a blank.

"Perhaps he stores things under the floorboards... no, that doesn't make sense," said Rachel, airing her thoughts. She leaned against a wall and closed her eyes, trying to go through in her mind all the places she had already looked. Having re-examined any possible locations she might have missed, she realised that the only remaining area left untouched, was the wall in the study that was covered by bookshelves.

Inside the study, she hurriedly removed the books from the shelves; carefully at first, but as her anxiety increased, she simply pulled them off, letting them fall to the floor. The piles of books mounted, until at last the small door of a safe was revealed. "Yes!" she screamed and punched the air like a footballer that had just scored in a cup final.

However, the ecstasy of finding the safe was short-lived, as it was locked and required a code to be punched in to unlock it. Still, she had crossed one bridge in finding it and maybe she could cross this one as well. Rachel knew that there was no certainty that the strange little box, if there really was another one, would be in there. Nevertheless, at least there had to be a chance.

She set to work straight away, typing in dates of birthdays. When that didn't succeed, she tried inputting them backwards or even jumbled out of sequence. With the most predictable number sequences failing to crack the code, she tried numbers in the titles of books from the Professor's shelves, such as George Orwell's '1984' and even a book of '1001 Recipes' but to no avail. Rachel sat down in the Professor's chair and tried to get into the Professor's mind, to think how he might think. This led to her trying the dates of birth and death of his heroes: Darwin and Newton. She even tried the registration year of his beloved 'Flying Spur'.

Again she was forced to return home without the box, but at least she was potentially just one number sequence from it. However, the probability of guessing the correct number, as she was very aware, was incredibly small. She didn't even know how long the number required was. Rachel considered again whether she should get someone else involved – and decided to do so if she couldn't crack the code by the end of the following day. She wondered how she would explain what had happened, especially if it turned out that there wasn't another box in the safe.

By evening time, Rachel had come to an acceptance that this was something she couldn't deal with alone. She lay on her bed, not tired, but lacking in motivation to do anything. After all, she had already tried everything she could think of. As she rested and drifted into that place between wakefulness and sleep, words came to her remembrance, words that were familiar – but in a different context:

'Here is wisdom. Let him that hath understanding count the number of the beast: for it is the number of a man; and his number is six hundred threescore and six.'

Rachel was at once fully awake, in her heart hoping that an answer had come but mostly believing that it was a trick of the mind. Turning to the book of Revelation in her Bible, she found the words that had just come to her, in the thirteenth chapter. She read through those particular verses a couple of times before putting it down on her bed.

Sitting down at her desk, she took a piece of paper from her folder and began writing the twenty-six letters of the English alphabet. She put a number beside each, one for A, two for B, three for C, four for D, etc.

If the Professor had used numbers that corresponded to a name of a person, then Rachel needed to guess which. Then there was also the nagging doubt that it would be just typical of the Professor, if he'd jumbled the numbers, or even used another alphabet...

Rachel decided on trying just two names: Andrew and Jacob. If those were incorrect then to keep on trying, she thought, would be like trying to find a needle in a haystack or getting the same number on a dice seven times in a row.

The numbers for Andrew were 1, 14, 4, 18, 5, & 23. For Jacob they were 10, 1, 3, 15, & 2.

With second thoughts, Rachel decided that it would be wise to work out the number for their surname 'Ketterley' as well. Her fluctuating expectations were quite low by this stage, but she felt that she owed it to Jacob to try.

Once again, Rachel was alone at Number 87, still wondering how she was going to explain all that had gone on as she typed in the first set of numbers. Nothing happened, the second set also failed, as did the numbers corresponding with the letters for Ketterley.

The one good aspect was that her failed attempts had not set off an alarm, but this was of little comfort. Rachel crumpled up the piece of paper, threw it across the room and then slumped down in a corner. She didn't want to get up, and she didn't want to stay there either. Her motivation was sapped by the overwhelming feeling of frustration.

After a time that seemed longer than it actually was, Rachel returned down the stairs and began to turn the key in the front door. "Oh, one more try," she sighed as she paused there for a moment before trudging back up to the study.

The door of the safe unlocked with a click this time as soon as she had entered the digits for 'Andrew', causing her to leap wildly with delight. She must have entered the numbers incorrectly the first time – but that didn't matter now. The thick steel door of the safe was now open to reveal various papers, a bundle of bank notes and, most importantly... a small cedar box.

Rachel held her treasured prize up to the wall light by the window. It certainly looked very old; she recognised the carving of a seven-branched lamp stand as being a Jewish 'Menorah'. Her mother had been given one as a gift in reward for time spent working in Haifa. What was puzzling to Rachel was how this interesting and unusual box could do anything. It had dials that turned the numbers around, some levers and buttons. But how could it cause time travel? ...any more than an alarm clock could, or anything else?

Her elation was now being challenged by the fear of the unknown. What if she couldn't get back again? What about her mum, dad and sister? She loved them dearly and couldn't bear to hurt them. She sat down at the Professor's desk, and, finding a notepad, she began to compose a letter. Rachel wrote in an attempt to explain what had happened and what she was going to do. She ended the letter with a message of thankfulness and love for her family – if they were to ever read these words.

Rachel began to tremble as she put on the backpack, feeling genuinely scared now by what might happen. The wheels of the Time Mechanism began to turn in one shaking hand as the fingers from the other set the digits. She set the twelve numbers on the front of the box at 1687 with eight zeros preceding it, presuming those windows to be for the year.

Not knowing what day to set, she turned the dials on the left of the carving until 'zero' and 'one' appeared in the windows. On the right, she set the numbers to 'zero' and 'seven' for July. Rachel wasn't entirely sure if she had set it correctly, as no one had shown her how to work the device – if it could be described as such. Pausing for a few minutes, she studied the settings intensely, trying to satisfy herself that they actually represented her chosen time destination and not something else. That place of certainty didn't come. Nevertheless, Rachel began pulling the levers and pressing the buttons at random.

The wood panelled walls and furnishings that surrounded her were replaced in an instant, with the purest white light. Clearly she had not arrived in Godstone 1687, but Rachel felt no fear that things had gone wrong, nor in fact any fear of any kind. The light was all encompassing, even beneath her feet there was only light and yet she was supported, as if still standing on the floor and able to walk around.

Rachel felt she could just stay in that place forever. Even if she just stood there and did nothing else, the peace and joy would have been enough. (She did stay there for a quite awhile, longer than she realised, and yet it was not measured in our time). Laying the Time Mechanism on the 'floor', she began walking ahead in a straight line for what she considered a few minutes. She saw nothing and no one, but the light. Strangely enough, despite not seeing anyone she felt she wasn't alone, as if in a crowd but without being able to see or touch those around her. Rachel even wondered if she had died and that might explain what was going on, or perhaps that she had been injured somehow, and was experiencing a hallucination...

The latter thought was soon dismissed; she was in a place beyond anyone's imagination. It reminded her a little of reading the 'Magician's Nephew' as a child. In that story, the children entered a different world with the aid of their 'magic' rings, only evil had no foothold where she was now. Coincidentally, the Professor even shared his name with one of the characters.

"There is something about this…" she said out loud as she repeatedly raised her hands into the light and then brought them back down to her sides in sweeping circles. "It's like a taste of something even better to come, a place of… encouragement."

A time arrived or at least a point, when Rachel knew she had to leave 'Encouragement', as she perceived it to be, and continue her journey. She didn't want to leave, but her senses were sharper there. Her mind was so clear that she had an inner 'knowing' of what was happening and what she must do. Rachel turned to walk back to where she had left the time mechanism, only to find it at her feet. Kneeling down to pick it up, she realised the digits were not as she had set them, but instead were a complete row of sevens. Rachel couldn't understand how that could be; she was certain that wasn't her doing. Moving the wheels again, the dates aligned once more at 1687. Understanding now the correct procedure, she began moving the levers and then pressed the buttons again…

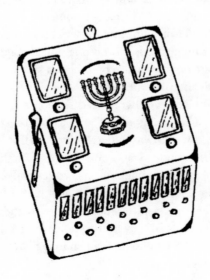

Chapter Seven

Highwaymen

Well, they had been lucky. From their sudden departure at the dining table of Number 87, they had fallen just a few inches onto a patch of grass, amongst a cluster of trees. Jacob realised straight away the dangers they had avoided. So close had they been to 'appearing' in the same spot as one of the nearby pines or towering oaks.

"Come on boy, let's go. I desire swiftly to find thine uncle and forever leave this place... or time. Trenchie ain't cut out for this life no more – it's the future for me."

The pirate strode out from amongst the woodland towards a track, rutted by cart wheels and hoof prints. Jacob found it bizarre that someone from the past, who hadn't even experienced electricity, could have felt so at home in the twenty- first century. Trenchie, however, was an adventurer by nature and to him, time was just another foreign land to be explored – and exploited.

After a few minutes of brisk walking, sometimes breaking into a jog, Trenchie came to a stop. He looked behind, then around him with one hand supporting his chin, the fingers scratching his beard. "Odd that, boy."

"This whole thing is odd, what do you mean?"

"I believed I knew where we were. But we cannot be... there should be a cottage here and there is not." Trenchie was still in possession of the Time Mechanism and holding it away from Jacob as he read the date settings, he let out a flurry of swear words. The furious pirate turned, looked straight at Jacob and said through clenched teeth: "We be in 1554... now why should that be, what didst thou bring us here for?"

"I didn't, I set it at 1687, why would I want to go to 1554 when my uncle's in 1687?"

That did make sense to Trenchie, although he wasn't prepared to acknowledge it. "Well I'll do it this time, thou know'st not how to work it."

As he pulled levers and pressed buttons in every combination, he cursed in his anger and acted as if to throw the small cedar box. However, the knowledge of its importance restrained him from doing so. They remained right there in 1554 despite every effort, with the brass wheels rotating back every time he attempted to change the year

"What be the meaning of this?" thundered Trenchie.

Jacob thought about making a run for it. The pirate was really losing control and he still had the loaded pistols. Jacob managed to make a stand though, not wishing to be away from the time mechanism.

"It's never done that before, honest, let's just give it a bit of time, perhaps we've done something wrong, or it just needs a rest..."

"Rest? ... It's a box, not an 'orse."

"Just give it a bit of time. Anyway, you're not far from your own time, you can survive in this culture."

It really was a time much the same as the pirate's own. The fifteen hundreds were hard to distinguish from the sixteen hundreds or the preceding centuries. The lifestyle of the poor differed little, transport was by foot, horse or wooden ship, and heat by open fires – the difference being in the names, faces and the politics.

"Right, boy, thou art to get the box working... at least,

thou better had. But for now, we need to get us some grub, and that means money, and that means robbing."

"We'll be hung!" Jacob protested, not fancying siding with Trenchie against the rest of the world.

"Gotta catch us first, boy. Now let us find some travellers, they're easy pickings. The villagers don't have much anyway and they're a lot more dangerous – they stick together."

Jacob soon began to feel hungry as they made their way through farm and woodland, sometimes along well-worn paths, but mostly not. They stayed away from the houses and inns for the time being, keeping out of sight of the locals to avoid attracting any attention. Strangers were always the talk of such places, as people travelled rarely and mostly for only short distances.

The steeple of the St. Nicholas' church building was a welcome sight as it towered above the trees. Familiarity was somehow comforting and gave Jacob hope that he would find his way home again. After what seemed a long time, they came across a stream and took the opportunity to drink and rest.

"Where are we?"

"Tilburstow Hill. Just beyond the trees over there is the road. We sometimes bring goods up from the coast to Croydon along there – but not all the time, mind. Only fools use the same route twice in a row, and they soon find themselves on a different road," said Trenchie chillingly "...to the gallows."

"Goods? You mean smuggling contraband."

"I'm guilty of much wrong, it is true – but the smuggling I am proud of. Maybe I should not have done some of the things I did under Captain Morgan... but the poor – the poor do well out of smugglers. We help the poor; we get 'em things that their lordships never would. I make more money from smuggling than I did from piracy, and it makes other folk happy as well... apart from the Crown – but they don't do anything for the likes of me. My father fought for the first King

Charles. The gentry did nothing for us when he met his death... but smugglers, we look after our own," said Trenchie with a certain amount of pride.

Jacob wasn't totally convinced by Trenchie's claims of altruism, but his fierce companion was at least showing signs of humanity, though like us all, of a fallen one. As they sat on the sun-baked earth, untouched by a nearby flowing stream, Jacob again tried the Time Mechanism. As before, he was only to find its wheels rotate backwards until 1554 was reached. He tried other dates before and after 1554, but no matter which date was inputted, the result was the same.

"Do you think we are in control of this thing, Trenchie, or is it taking us where it wants?"

"Why dost thou ask me? Art thou not the one with the magic lights and sounds that come from nowhere?"

"That's not magic, those things at home are things people make and they are powered by electricity. Everything has a natural explanation," declared Jacob.

"Magic or electricity, it be all the same to me. If that thing's not magic..." Trenchie said, pointing towards the Time Mechanism, "Then how does it work?"

Jacob couldn't answer, he knew logically that this wooden box couldn't cause time travel, that it shouldn't be able to do anything much, apart from store a few small items. Yet here they were, existing in a different time, defying all rational explanation.

"See, boy, thou art no Isaac Newton. If thou canst explain all things, then tell me of how the Earth, Moon and stars were made?"

"We call it the Big Bang."

"The what? The only 'Big Bang' Trenchie ever heard was from the mouth of a cannon and I can tell thee it made nothing good. You future folk have strange ideas, bewitched most likely."

As they sat there comparing worldviews, they began to

hear voices in the distance. Trenchie got to his feet and drew a flintlock pistol from his belt. From among the bushes bordering the road, they could see two horses pulling a cart, driver atop, and two horsemen behind it. Trenchie studied the horsemen to see how they were armed; one had an arquebus – an early type of rifle, used until they were superseded by muskets. The other, larger figure had a sword, a ring-hilted one, which defined him as a 'Gallowglass' – an Irish mercenary and a formidable foe.

"They be smugglers, boy. This route has been used for years," said the excited Trenchie, now in his element.

Jacob found it strange that they should arrive at Tilburstow Hill just as the smugglers arrived and wondered at the coincidence of it. "There's three of them Trenchie and they're armed – what are you going to do?"

"Three of them... and I've got three shooters. I'll take the big fella first, he be a mercenary, if I miss him we shall be in dead trouble."

"If you kill them, you'll draw every soldier for miles to Godstone to hunt us down."

This wasn't the sort of advice Trenchie was used to and he chose to ignore it. As the cart drew alongside their position, Trenchie leapt from the bushes, a pistol in each hand.

"Stand and deliver!" the pirate-turned-smuggler, and now highwayman, shouted. Jacob, who had remained in the cover of the foliage, just rolled his eyes.

"He thinks he's Dick Turpin now!" Jacob muttered under his breath as he wriggled backwards, further into the green covering.

The Gallowglass reached for his sword, but froze as Trenchie aimed one pistol in his direction. "Now me, lads, I'm one of you and am needing your help. A few coins to tide me over while I sort a few things out, that's all I ask."

"Three of us, one of thee... think thou may'st have taken

on a bit too much, old man?" came the sneering retort from the tousled haired driver. The 'arquebusier' on the horse took aim at Trenchie, only to be felled by a shot that thudded into his shoulder, dismounting him from his horse.

The Gallowglass charged sword in hand, only to be met with the butt of Trenchie's pistol as it was flung through the air. Stunned for a moment but still mounted, the Gallowglass composed himself for another attack. However, not before another of Trenchie's pistols flashed, leaving a strong smell of sulphur and another horseman prostrate on the ground.

"Don't make me kill ye, just let me take my spoils, and ye can go on yer way. There be an inn up ahead where ye can have yer wounds made good. Now mark this, there be no need to talk of us, and we shall have no want of mentioning yer little journeys to and fro from the coast, now, shall we? Come out now, Jakey, and see what they've got."

Jacob hadn't really wanted to get involved, but his future now seemed tied to that of the old pirate. The two wounded men stayed on the ground, realising that further resistance was pointless. Trenchie still had one more loaded pistol and by no means looked reluctant to use it.

The cart contained boxes filled with tobacco, bottles of spirits and bundles of fine silks. Jacob felt guilty as he took some of the contraband from the cart, as well as clothing which would fit him – and which would allow him to blend into his new surroundings. He knew that Trenchie would be able to make money selling the contraband goods... and after all, they were hungry, he reasoned. Jacob tried to justify their actions in his mind by telling himself that these people were criminals and that therefore, the goods weren't legally theirs either.

When Trenchie decided that they had what they needed, the cart was allowed to make its way along the road. The wounded men needed treatment, and they were in no mood for a fight. They meekly clambered into the back of the cart and lay down in the space vacated by the removal of the goods. The arquebus was now in Jacob's possession, as was the sword, leaving the scowling driver no choice but to crack the whip and leave the scene.

"Not bad for an old man, eh, boy?" grinned the triumphant Trenchie. As he raised a bottle of rum to his lips to toast his victory, he boasted: "It'll take more than the likes of them to bring down this old pirate."

"You really enjoyed that, didn't you?"

"I did that boy, I did that – but I'd be enjoying things a lot more if we could get back to thy time." Trenchie was satisfied for now, however. He felt he had proven himself in this new time. Trenchie felt comfortable with reactions of fear from those around him, actually revelling in it. He could stand anything but indifference – and if he was forced to spend time in 1554, he was determined to make his mark.

Rain began to fall, and Jacob set about tying the various boxes and bundles to the arquebusier's horse, with rope and sheets of cloth. Once everything was secure, Trenchie mounted the Irish mercenary's horse, leaving Jacob to guide the 'pack horse' on foot.

They were soon in the village of Godstone, with Trenchie feeling like a conquering General. His majestic, well-groomed black stallion trotted along the cobblestone road to the familiar sight of the 'White Hart' inn – or 'Clayton Arms', as it was called at one time.

"It'll be good for us in the White Hart, Jakey. The law was never welcome in there if thou know'st what I mean."

They made their way to the rear of the building where a bald-headed, well-fed looking man was standing – as if already expecting them.

"Art thou Porter?" enquired Trenchie still on horseback.

"Who wants to know?"

"What year be it?" Trenchie asked.

"Eh? 1554, of course... art thou mocking me?" replied the man angrily.

"That's right, and it was thy great grandson who told me about thee, thou conniving rogue. But never mind that – we want to do some business."

Ernest Porter looked suitably confused by their conversation – not surprising, as he was only forty and had no grandchildren, let alone a great grandson. "Show me thy wares thou old jester, what hast thou got for us?"

Porter had been expecting the smugglers who Trenchie had robbed at Tilburstow Hill. He wasn't too interested anyway in who brought the goods, in fact he preferred not to get too involved with them. He never asked them where they were from, or their names. Actually, names were best not mentioned in case there were any informers about. As landlord at the White Hart, he made a lot of money buying from smugglers and then selling the goods to customers. Occasionally, even some soldiers would come to buy contraband or take some free – in order to keep their lips shut tight about what was going on there.

After a few minutes of haggling over prices, a consensus was reached. Porter knew better than to insult these apparent 'smugglers' by offering too little and Trenchie dared not ask for too much, as they urgently needed the money. Porter also offered the use of one of the rooms at the White Hart into the bargain, which they gladly accepted.

The room itself was small, with a leaded window facing the rear, overlooking the woods. The oak-beamed ceiling was only a foot above Trenchie's head – but then, he was a tall man. Jacob fell back onto one of the two beds with a big sigh. It had been a tiring day in every sense, and no matter what future awaited them – at least for a while, he could get some rest. He was feeling a bit more comfortable in Trenchie's company now, though not completely.

Jacob felt the old pirate at least accepted him as 'one of his men', especially in the absence of his gang of smugglers, once fifteen men strong. Some had had military experience, and the others had been criminals of various kinds. Individually wild and ill-disciplined – with Trenchie in charge, they had been a formidable unit.

"Look, Jake, mate – we got off to a bad start, lad, but I think we can work together. I allow not an armed man to stand near me, if he has not my trust."

Jacob had been allowed to take the weapons from the three smugglers at Tilburstow Hill, but he hadn't thought of using them. He most certainly hadn't contemplated taking on Trenchie with either sword or gun. He knew Trenchie, though ageing, was still more than competent in the use of weapons. Jacob was also aware from his studies of local history that 'Trenchie' or John Edward Trenchman, to give him his full name, was the only surviving smuggler at the battle of Tilburstow Hill... though the records told that he was to die from his wounds shortly after. Now, they were in a different century from where that event had taken place. He wondered whether that fate would still await Trenchie, or if history itself had been altered. However, was that even possible?

The situation seemed mind-boggling. Jacob knew that in science fiction stories, history couldn't be changed – but he couldn't be sure those stories were right. This was for real, people had actual weapons that could do you damage, and the smells and tastes were more vivid than even the most eloquent fiction writer could describe.

As Jacob began to drift toward sleep, he closed his eyes and prayed that he would see his uncle and Rachel at least one more time. The Professor always ridiculed the concept of God, but Rachel seemed sure of her beliefs. Jacob hoped that Rachel was the one who was right... and that there would be an answer to his plea.

Chapter Eight

Manasseh

When Jacob and Trenchie had left 2011, it had been summer. However, in 1554, the time in which they had arrived against their will, it was the beginning of winter. Three weeks after their arrival at the White Hart, the temperature had dropped noticeably.

They had tried to use the time mechanism every day – at least half a dozen times a day, to be more precise, but still without success. It seemed that, the more they tried unsuccessfully to operate that little old cedar box, the more precious it became. All their hopes and dreams seemed focussed upon it.

Jacob thought that Trenchie should be reasonably content, as, after all, Godstone in 1554 was little different to his own time, apart from the people. However, the old pirate also felt very much a stranger in a strange land, despite the familiarity of many of the buildings. More than that, now that Trenchie had had a glimpse of the distant future, he could no longer feel satisfied until he had it in his grasp.

The money made from selling the items they took from the smugglers was enough for the time being. Trenchie supplemented it by catching the odd rabbit or two. He also made money by gambling at the White Hart at night. Trenchie was especially successful at a card game called 'Primero', which he had learned on his travels. The old pirate always seemed to win when he needed to – usually losing a couple of games for small money and then winning when an opponent increased the stakes, encouraged by his earlier victories. It was suspicious to say the least, but rumours about Trenchie's actions at Tilburstow Hill had put people off challenging him.

Jacob would spend most evenings alone by a window near the entrance overlooking the horse pond. It was a familiar sight to him, but there were no ducks there. If there had been, they would probably have ended up on someone's dinner table. The surface of the pond was frozen hard, making Jacob extremely grateful to be in the warmth of the inn.

He kept himself to himself, partly because he found it hard, at times, to have conversations – as the English spoken then was a bit different to the modern version. Actually, quite a number of the people thought he was a foreigner and so regarded him as something of a curiosity. Thankfully, though, for Jacob, he was spared some awkward questions about who he was and what he was doing there, as Trenchie's larger-than-life personality drew most of the attention to the pirate.

One particularly cold night, Jacob was sitting down in his usual place. A large chunk of bread and a piece of cheese were his meal on an old pine trestle table before him. He was starting to enjoy his basic but fresh diet and was observing history alive before his eyes – but most of all, he enjoyed the heat from the fire that crackled in the brick hearth.

He closed his eyes for a few moments, deliberately imagining that he was still in 2011 and that Rachel and his uncle were there with him. After all, they were separated by time rather than great distance. Jacob could see, in his mind's eye, the cars that would occasionally be driving past the window, people whom he knew, or faces he just recognised. Such ordinary sights, though, only conjured in his mind, now took on an altogether more wondrous image to Jacob than anything he had seen in his 'travels'.

The warm feelings engendered by his dreams began to dissipate, as worry again began to eat them away. He thought about his uncle and wondered how he was coping in 1687. Perhaps they were sitting in the exact same spot, but separated by about a hundred and thirty three years. Perhaps things weren't going so well for him – perhaps he'd had to resort to begging to survive. Maybe he had left Godstone, and then, how would Jacob find him? If he didn't know *where* he was, but knew *when*, then...

Jacob's wandering mind was brought back to his immediate surroundings by gentle taps on the window. He saw a group of children peering through the glass, gesturing for him to join them. The cold outside wasn't very appealing, and he thought they were probably beggars – but he couldn't ignore them.

"Art thou Jacob, sir?" asked a smiling girl of about five years, wearing a brown felt hat that was far too big.

"Er, yes... how do you know my name, and who are you?"

"My name is Josie."

Shyness overcame her, so one of the older children in the group, a boy, took over.

"Anna and Josie believed thou wast him... we were not so sure. But thou art not like any of us and thou talk'st unusual, sir, like as Miss Rachel."

"Callum!" exclaimed Anna, the slightly older of the two girls, as she tried to pull her cousin away. "We should not be here, Mummy will tell us off."

"No, no, please don't go... this 'Miss Rachel', what does she look like?"

"She's from a faraway land, sir. Her skin is of a different hue, not seen the like of her around here before. But she is kind, sir, and she needs thee," explained a boy called Stephen.

Jacob shivered, but not from the cold. Surely, he thought, Rachel had found the other time mechanism and had followed after him. He desperately wanted to see her and just get out of this time.

"Please take me to her... I'll pay you – please, where is she?" he pleaded, rather unnecessarily.

"We've got to take Daniel back to Mum!" demanded Anna of the others, as she held the hand of the youngest of the group of five.

"Forgive us, sir, but the hour is late and we must leave. Go thou to the church building of 'St. Nicholas', she spends much time there," suggested Stephen as the little group turned to leave.

"Thank you, thank you so much... please, take this." Jacob thrust all the coins he had into the hand of the oldest child, not expecting to have any further use for them. Then he turned and ran down the lane leading to the church building. He couldn't believe that Rachel had been so close, and he wondered when she had arrived.

A pain developed in his chest as he inhaled large gulps of cold air. Jacob passed the water mill on his left and the large pond that serviced it. He could hear the sound of animals scuttling through the bushes in the darkness, disturbed by his presence. A few hundred metres more, and the old church building came into view. The sight of candlelight from its windows filled Jacob with renewed hope.

Jacob tripped as he rushed up the steps to the churchyard, such was his hurry... then, back on his feet, he ran towards the door of the church, slowing to a more respectful jog as he reached it. Jacob felt a lump in his throat as he gazed into the inadequately lit interior – which barely differed from how it had been at the carol service. It seemed to connect him to his own time and to how he wished he could be there again.

Reverend James Manasseh was surprised to see Jacob enter the building; it was late, and he had never seen this young man there before.

"Thou art welcome, sir, but the hour is late, may I ask what brings thee here this cold evening?"

"Excuse me, Reverend, I heard that a friend of mine might be here; perhaps you may know where she is... her name's Rachel, she..."

"Rachel Isaacson? Thou must be Jacob; thine accent is like hers also. She is a graceful young woman; she gave me new insights into the scriptures, such that I felt as if I myself had been there on the road to Emmaus. I fear, though, for her safety, sir – the young lady is incautious and in great danger." With that, the forty-something, stocky cleric hurried down the aisle and bolted the heavy oak doors of the building.

"Where is she, and what do you mean by danger?"

"Thou appear'st to be English, but for thy curious way of speaking... and yet, like Rachel, thou dost not seem to know what has been happening. Queen Mary is trying to stop all people from using the Prayer Book, yet Rachel has travelled to attend a secret prayer meeting. A farm labourer called John Launder and the carpenter Thomas Iveson are those that are escorting her. I warned her not to go... I tried to tell her."

It was hard for Jacob to appreciate how a prayer meeting could put you in danger, as he thought it was something only little old ladies attended. However, from his history studies, he was aware of Queen Mary's infamous nickname, 'Bloody Mary'. He knew that the vicar was not exaggerating.

The rugged vicar suddenly clasped his hands to his face and groaned loudly.

"It is my fault...", he eventually whispered, removing his hands and with tears in his eyes. "It is I who am the betrayer..."

"What do you mean? What's going on?!"

"I've betrayed them, Jacob, like Judas – but not for money... I was for burning... I couldn't face the fire; the soldiers were here, and, wretched man that I am, I betrayed my friends."

Jacob was shocked at hearing all this and thought that he should be angry, even violent towards the broken-hearted cleric. Instead, he felt pity – and, putting his hands on the older man's shoulders gently but firmly, he said, "What's done is done... please help me find her, and you can put all this right."

"I know not if I can, but I will try to make this thing right. If it had been anything but the fire..."

"Please, Reverend, we must hurry!"

"Yes, yes... thou art right, of course." Reverend Manasseh was so stricken by guilt and shame; he couldn't bear to look Jacob in the eyes. He led Jacob into the vestry, where he took a map from a shelf and unrolled it upon a table.

"They left yesterday. Rachel has been staying in the home of Ruth, the sister of John Launder, since her recent arrival. They are gathering with others in the village of Foxe, near Brighton. They shall be tarrying there this night and tomorrow. They will be safe this night, but not tomorrow, for when the full number has come in, the Queen's men will seize them."

"Then we must get there in time... Do you have any horses?"

"Follow me, but make no sound."

With that, Reverend Manasseh blew out a candle and carefully opened the rear door of the vestry. In silence, he led Jacob down the steps and through the graveyard. Manasseh looked around, as if expecting to find someone watching – not that they could see much in the darkness. At the end of the graveyard, they found their way to a path through the adjoining field, the only light being that of a full moon and the company of distant stars. The path took them to a large barn. "I believe we have not been discovered. In here are kept the finest horses in the parish – at least, that is my consideration."

Once inside, Manasseh went about lighting the tallow candles, which were randomly situated within the old barn. In the dim light Jacob could see three 'Great Horses', similar to the modern Shire breed. They looked majestic, well groomed and all black in colour, but for the white markings on their faces and feet. However, with their powerful but heavy bodies, Jacob wondered how quickly they would get them to Foxe village. Having been told what fine creatures they were, he was half-expecting to see racehorses – but at least, these could be relied upon to get them to their destination.

One thing Jacob had omitted to mention was that he had never ridden a horse in his life. He thought it best to keep that knowledge to himself and waited as Reverend Manasseh finished saddling the two chosen for the journey. Manasseh gave their necks a good scratch, which they seemed to enjoy. He led them alongside a mounting block made up of odd bits of masonry. Jacob confidently put his left foot into the iron stirrup and, with reins in one hand, proceeded to mount – only for his horse to swing away, leaving him flat on his back on the floor of the barn.

Manasseh looked bewildered, not sure what to make of this young man, who with the exception of Rachel seemed so different to anyone else that he'd ever encountered. He concluded that Jacob must have been a bit drunk. "Perhaps, I think, it would be best if I helped thee mount," he advised diplomatically.

Jacob, who was by now back on his feet, nodded and mumbled a humble, "Yes, please."

Reverend Manasseh held the horse still as Jacob again put his foot in the stirrup and, with one hand holding the reins and the other on the saddle's cantle, hauled himself up until he was sitting high and upright. From the barn, they made their way to the High Road that would take them on their journey south. Once his horse had begun to trot, Jacob found it quite easy to ride, as his horse followed the lead of Manasseh and his mount.

The cold was biting, and flakes of snow had begun to fall by the time they had completed the first three miles. As they journeyed on, Jacob considered that he had never experienced such bitter weather. With the centrally heated homes and cars of his time, he had never had to spend a long period facing the elements. The wind was no friend either, as it drove the snowflakes, which seemed larger than in the winters he had experienced, into their faces. As he shivered violently on his saddle, he remembered stories of terrible winter journeys – from Hannibal's Carthaginians crossing the Alps to the incursions into Russia of the armies of Napoleon and Hitler.

They forced themselves onwards – five miles, ten miles, fifteen miles and then twenty miles – Manasseh driven by guilt and the hope of redeeming the situation, Jacob by the hope of seeing Rachel again. Living in a different time period seemed to Jacob rather like living alone on a deserted island. Though he was surrounded by people, he felt lonely just the same. Jacob prayed in his heart that they would get there in time – and in fact, also to simply survive the night.

"Reverend!" called Jacob, as his horse came to a halt, his hands so cold that he could no longer even hold the reins. "I can't go on. You must go without me and find Rachel."

"I cannot leave thee, Jacob; there is a place not three miles hence, where there is both warmth and safe lodgings for the night. Thou must not tarry here."

They carried on for another few miles, Reverend Manasseh now guiding Jacob's horse by its reins. Just off the road, they came to what was now a snow-covered track which led them to some farm buildings. Manasseh dismounted and walked to the door of a small cottage with windows shuttered to keep out the freezing night air, his legs feeling stiff and his toes numb.

Knocking loudly on the door, he waited as the inhabitants made themselves ready, not expecting visitors at such an unusual hour. After what seemed to be a long while, which everything did out in the cold, the door finally opened to reveal a grey-haired man holding a sword, in the doorway.

"Reverend Manasseh... be thou here? What dost thou here at this hour? Come in, sir, before the cold has thee... and thy friend there," he said, gesturing towards the figure of Jacob, who was still on horseback.

The farmer, Alan Tiller, went to help Jacob dismount and took him inside the cottage, where his wife, Frances, was busy lighting a fire. Reverend Manasseh took the horses into the shelter of a barn where he was able to feed and water them. Even inside the relative warmth of the cottage, Jacob continued to shiver uncontrollably and was more than grateful to be served a bowl of warm soup.

"The Queen has sent some men to Foxe, to capture dissenters who still use the old Prayer Book. It is our most earnest desire to reach them first and give warning," explained Manasseh as the four of them sat around the fireplace.

"Thou art a brave man, good on thee, sir!" said Mrs Tiller, adding only to the guilt Manasseh felt.

Jacob, having finished his soup, felt compelled to challenge them, "Religion causes so much trouble," he stated abruptly.

Mr and Mrs Tiller were quite taken aback by Jacob's words. They were used to people taking a partisan position on the Protestant or Catholic side, but not criticising both.

"Some take up the cause of the Lord because they do truly believe in Him. Others do so because they wish to misuse it in order to gain power and wealth among the uneducated. Still others are simply misguided and misled – it has been much the case for centuries," said Manasseh sadly. "They persecute people for supposed heresy, while claiming to follow the one who said: 'love your enemies'. Now that be the utmost wickedness... the dear ones at Foxe are as lilies amongst the thorns; they harm no man, and yet they draw the wrath of man upon themselves."

Reverend Manasseh's words were eloquent, but had the unintended effect of increasing Jacob's fears. He knew Rachel didn't deserve such a fate, especially given that she was passionately opposed to religious bigotry. Anyway, this wasn't her battle, he thought to himself – now even more determined to get to Foxe to rescue her.

"We've got to get to Rachel, I'm fine now... thank you for your hospitality, but we must go!" Jacob said, rising to his feet.

"Rest now, my friend, the soldiers will strike not until our friends have gathered in one place. Thou must rest and thy horse also, then leave at first dawn with our blessing," came the quiet but authoritative words of the farmer.

Jacob knew that his host was right. His body ached after the long ride, and it was becoming increasingly difficult to keep his eyelids open. He was shown to a bed in the adjoining room, luxurious compared to the one at the White Hart. It even had a pillow, the first to rest his head on since he had left 2011.

Despite his willingness, hours earlier, to continue the journey, it was Manasseh who had to wake him, eager to move on. The fire had long since gone out, and the room felt very cold even to Jacob, who was fully clothed. The Tillers gave them some bread, cheese and water for the journey and then said their goodbyes. The farmer and his wife tried to hide their feelings of concern for their friend and his young companion as they waved them off. They were in unforgiving times, and not many could be deemed safe, at least not in the temporal world.

Chapter Nine

Unless a Grain of Wheat Falls

The snow had relented, as had the wind, as they set off. Jacob had never had any pets apart from a guinea pig, when he was small. However, he was now growing quite fond of this horse. As he rode, he began to imagine himself heroically riding to Rachel's rescue – and then the two of them galloping off together through the fields. From time to time, these thoughts of chivalry were replaced with doubts as to whether they would get there before it was too late. As the hours passed and they drew closer to their destination, Jacob started to feel 'butterflies' in his stomach. The fear of how he would react if the soldiers arrested him now occupied his thoughts.

Reverend Manasseh had also considered what might happen and had steeled himself to face whatever would await. There were no dreams of great deeds for him. He was only too aware of the reality of the situation.

As they came within a mile of Foxe, Manasseh brought his horse into a canter and rode down a track to the left of the road, with Jacob following suit. All worries seemed to vanish as they rode closer and closer, the adrenaline now overpowering their emotions. Jacob was by now quite confident in his horsemanship, and the power of his magnificent 'Great Horse' gave him some extra boldness. Clearing the trees that had flanked them on each side, the track took them through open fields and within sight of a small, picturesque village.

"God be with thee, Jacob!" shouted Manasseh as his horse began to gallop, leaving Jacob in his wake. Manasseh had at one time been a cavalryman – and he rode as one, dramatically pulling up outside a small church building in the centre of the village. He dismounted and, wasting no time at all, ran through the lychgate and past the people who were making their way up the path.

Inside the building were about forty people including children. Some were already seated on the wooden pews, while others mingled at the back, talking quietly. Jumping onto one of the wooden pews in the centre of the building, the cleric shouted a warning to his hearers: "Friends, ye be in the gravest of dangers. The Queen does know of this gathering, and her soldiers shall soon be upon us."

Manasseh felt purged of his guilt as he spoke, but his feeling of elation vanished as soon as he heard the shouts and screams of those who had remained outside. Jacob was by now in the centre of the village, still mounted, and could see horsemen fast approaching from the north of the village and also from the south. Around him, the frightened villagers were scattering in all directions, some carrying young children.

"Rachel! Rachel! Rachel…!" he shouted repeatedly, as he looked around for her. Congregants streamed out of the church building, with Manasseh the last to leave. Soldiers with crested helmets and pikes appeared from the far side of the churchyard, forcing the people towards the front, to where the horsemen were advancing.

"Jake!" called a voice he hadn't heard for what seemed like forever.

Rachel came running towards him, with a soldier not far behind her and quickly gaining ground. She was grabbed by the hair, just as she reached her hand up to Jacob, and was pulled violently to the ground. As Jacob was about to dismount, the soldier was himself knocked to the ground by Manasseh.

"Get her away, my friend!" he urged, as he helped Rachel onto the back of the horse. Manasseh tried to run to his own steed, only for the grounded soldier to grab his left boot. He tried to kick him off, but by now three more soldiers with pikes were surrounding him.

"Leave him alone!" shouted Jacob in despair.

"Get the wench!" ordered one of the bearded troops. Jacob knew he could not help Manasseh and spurred his horse into a gallop through the middle of a group of soldiers – who were forced to jump out of the way.

Rachel hugged Jacob tight, wanting to say so much – but at the same time worried for the safety of her new friends. All such thoughts were immediately replaced by terror, as the sound of hoof-beats grew loud behind them. Two horsemen, swords drawn, were chasing after them, determined to stop their escape. The gap between them and their pursuers began to close as Jacob headed towards a wood where he hoped to lose them. The powerful but heavy horse, not yet rested from its long journey, began to tire. It allowed one of their pursuers to get within ten metres of them by the time they reached the enticing covering of trees. Jacob wished he had taken the arquebus with him, even if it was quite a primitive gun. Escape for them was now impossible.

"Halt or feel my blade!" ordered the first of the cavalrymen, as he finally drew alongside them on the brow of a hill.

With the other horseman close behind, Jacob had no real option but to bring his horse slowly to a halt. They were forced to dismount and made to walk on ahead of the two riders. One of the horsemen led Jacob's tired horse along behind him by its reins, as they headed back towards Foxe.

"I'm so sorry, Rachel, if only we hadn't stopped for the night, we could have saved you... and the others. I'll get you out of this somehow, I won't let you die here," Jacob promised, though with absolutely no idea as to how.

"I tried the time box or whatever you call it, but it won't work and not only that but we're in the wrong year – it's 1554 and your uncle is in 1687."

"Yeah, yeah. It's the same with my one. I thought Trenchie was going to kill me for not getting it to work, but he's been okay to be honest. I'm really, sorry, Rachel, that you've been caught up in all this. It was just fun at first, and there were no problems at all – not until this time journey."

"I had to find you, Jake. I'm not sorry I came... terrified, but not sorry."

"Rachel, if you get an opportunity to escape, you've got to take it and not worry about me. Think about your family, at home, and how they'd feel – if something happened to you. We've got to be realistic and accept that we might not both make it." Jacob gave Rachel a friendly wink and tried to appear calmer than he felt.

Once back in the village, they saw a horse-drawn cart containing Manasseh and four other men. A couple of soldiers armed with pikes – a type of spear about three metres in length – escorted them to the back of the cart where they were roughly made to clamber on. No one spoke until the driver of the cart cracked the whip and their journey commenced. They were not shackled, but with a dozen armed horsemen to the rear, they didn't need to be.

Most of the villagers stayed indoors, glad to have been allowed to return to their homes, but a few with solemn faces watched from their windows.

"We shall be happy for those of our friends that have been spared," said Manasseh, breaking the silence.

"Yes, better us than others," agreed another captive, nobly.

Jacob wondered if they meant what they said or were just trying to be positive. He rubbed his eyes as the figures of two of the captives seemed to blur momentarily, just as the Time Mechanism had, back in Wigglesworth Road. "My name is Jacob, and you are...?" he asked them.

The two men that had appeared to blur introduced themselves as John Launder and Thomas Iveson. Jacob thought he remembered those names from his studies as being the two 'Godstone Martyrs', but he wasn't sure. The remaining two prisoners were Jack Pullinger and Henry Pawson – two Sussex farmers.

"Where do you think they are taking us?" asked Rachel.

"London. No doubt we are to be tried before Bishop Bonner," said Iveson gently.

"A Bishop... well maybe if we just explain what we were doing, that we weren't doing anything wrong, then he'll understand and let us go," said Rachel, convincing no one including herself.

"Dear Rachel, if he be God's servant, then what thou say'st is correct – but I fear there are other powers who guide his decisions. Great is the darkness that covers the Earth, but it shall not always be this way," answered Launder enigmatically.

"There is something... I must confess..." stammered Reverend Manasseh.

"'Tis done, friend, do not burden thyself any longer," Launder said compassionately. Manasseh wasn't sure if they knew what he'd done, but said no more.

The bumpy ride in the four-wheeled cart wasn't a pleasant one. It had again turned bitterly cold, and more snow was falling. The view from the cart was like that of a classic winter scene on a Christmas card. However, with the circumstances in which Jacob and Rachel found themselves, they found the beauty hard to appreciate. They had not experienced such temperatures and heavy snow in England, but here in 1554 they were experiencing a foretaste of the 'Little Ice Age' that was to dominate the coming centuries.

The shivering little group of prisoners huddled closely together, trying to keep warm, as the cart slowly progressed along the road towards London. It was a road which would eventually take them back through Godstone on their way to their expected fate. They stopped at the village of 'Hoppestead', near a small river and the snow-blanketed fields of 'Creighton Heath'. The horses drank from a horse trough while some of the soldiers took the opportunity to get some refreshments and warmth at the inn.

The four remaining soldiers, or 'yeomen', had also dismounted and stood in a group talking, occasionally glancing over to their prisoners to make sure they didn't try to run.

"If it were in my power to do so, I would make ye free men... and women," whispered the driver of the cart, as he turned around and looked at the captives. "May I ask of ye to forgive my part in this?"

"We bear you no ill, do what thou must," said Manasseh magnanimously.

Jacob wished the cart driver would do something else entirely, such as crack the whip and try to make an escape but that was unrealistic – the cart would have soon been caught by the cavalrymen anyway.

The young driver may not have been able to set them free, but he was kind enough to give them some bread to eat while the soldiers weren't looking. After about half an hour, four of their guards left the inn to take the place of those who had stayed outside with the prisoners. Jacob hoped that they might be taken into the warm inn for some respite themselves, but it wasn't to be.

When the soldiers were rested, they carried on their way. It was desperately cold now, and that was perhaps more difficult for Jacob and Rachel to handle than for the others who were more used to a harsher way of life. As they neared the village of Lingfield, the soldiers decided to cease their journey for the day and rest there. The village had a small gaol called the 'Cage', used for temporarily holding minor offenders. The officer in charge deemed this a useful place to leave Jacob, Rachel and the others for the night.

The tiny brick-built prison was a welcome shelter, offering protection from the wind. Outside, the soldiers took turns guarding them, while the others enjoyed themselves at the nearby inn. As the seven captives huddled together (not that there was much space to do anything else), Rachel took the time mechanism from inside her coat. Her fingers were so numb from the cold that she could barely hold it.

Rachel had previously set the time mechanism for 2011 and tried to push the buttons and pull the levers in various combinations, hoping to cause their escape. She closed her eyes as she did so, hoping to see new surrounds as they opened – but instead, the darkness of the tiny cell remained.

Meanwhile, Jacob managed to shuffle his way through the shivering group until he sat next to her.

"At least your uncle's not been caught up in this, Jake," she said.

"Yeah, I hope he's not banging on about science where he is, or they'll think he's into witchcraft or something!"

"It's weird though, isn't it, to think that he could be near us, but separated from us by time? What do you think is wrong with these time boxes? Do we have to be in a certain place to use them?" asked Rachel.

"No, we've used them loads of times, all over the place. There is one difference though... do you remember how the

time mechanism blurred, just before Trenchie and I came here? Well, that had never happened before…"

"I did notice, but what does it mean?"

"I don't know, but if it happens again, we'd better touch the time mechanism quickly," advised Jacob.

Night came and the prisoners were cold, hungry and tired, but they couldn't sleep in these circumstances. The two men whose turn it was to stand guard were approaching the end of their shift and were concentrating more on keeping warm than on watching their prisoners.

Jacob, sitting at the back of the building, could see them through the narrow gaps between the iron bars in front of a small window in the door. As he sat there, he was the first to see another, taller figure rush at the guards, sending one to the ground with a heavy blow to the back of the head. The fallen yeoman was soon to be joined by his comrade before the alarm could be raised.

By now, the prisoners were on their feet. They could hear the jangling of keys, the thud of more punches... then the face of Trenchie appeared, peering through the grille into the darkness of the cell.

"Jakey... art thou in there, boy?"

"I'm here, please get us out of here!" called Jacob, who was ecstatic at the sight of the old pirate.

The door swung open and in the light of the moon, they could see the young driver of the cart, manoeuvring his vehicle towards them.

"I tried to bribe 'im, but he would not take the money – he just wanted to help," explained Trenchie as he nodded in the driver's direction.

Trenchie helped all seven of them climb onto the cart and then mounted his own horse, which was tethered nearby. As the wheels of the cart began to turn again, one of the soldiers, who was pretending to be unconscious, got to his feet and rang the little gaol's brass bell.

"Stop that!" demanded Trenchie, as he rode towards the guard.

The yeoman stopped ringing and fled into the darkness before Trenchie's fury would be unleashed on him. The other soldiers had heard the alarm, though, and soon came rushing out from the inn – but rather unprepared. Some were half drunk, others twice as much as that and not wearing their armour. Trenchie calmly sat in his saddle and aimed his pistols at his would-be assailants. One of the soldiers was hit in the arm as Trenchie fired. This shocked them – as pistols were rare then –, and they had neither firearms nor bows. Trenchie fired off two more shots, one hitting an ale-inspired yeoman, who was trying to charge with his pike, the other harmlessly thudding into the wall of the inn.

Then, with a loud shout, Trenchie charged at the group of soldiers wielding the sword he had taken from the Gallowglass. The soldiers threw themselves out of the way – and Trenchie, bringing his horse to a halt, stared back at them contemptuously before riding off after the cart.

The bewildered soldiers, now bereft of their prisoners, ran to where they had stabled their horses, only to find them cut loose and wandering about in the surrounding woodland.

"Search for the horses and armour up! The horseman shall you kill, but the others are to be taken alive... if possible," ordered the officer in charge.

The soldiers eventually managed to collect all the horses together and formed a column, two horses abreast. However, this time they were only ten in total, as the two wounded stayed behind at the inn. The chill of the night air and the knowledge that one of their enemies had a firearm helped bring about some sobriety amongst the troop. Upon the officer's command, they set off in pursuit, following the tracks the cart had carved into the snow.

The cart driver had set off down a track that led to the village of Crowhurst. Earlier in the day, he and his passengers had been travelling at quite a slow pace, but now they hurtled along as fast as they could. Trenchie by now had caught up with them, rather proud of himself for taking the role of hero instead of villain for a change.

"First the smugglers, now the... Queen's men. 1554 cannot handle old Trenchie, eh, boy?" the pirate bragged to Jacob.

It soon became apparent that the cart, although travelling at a frenetic pace, was no match for the speed of the cavalry pursuing them. On entering Crowhurst, Trenchie shouted to the driver, telling him to come to a stop. Once the wheels stood still, he commanded them all to be quiet and just to listen. For a brief time, they could hear nothing at all – apart from the usual sounds of wild animals scuttling around... but they were dismayed to eventually hear the unmistakable rumble of horses in the distance.

"It is no good, we cannot outrun them. Driver, we shall make our escape on foot. Take the cart from here as far as possible without capture, and then save thyself," instructed Trenchie with authority.

The seven got down from the cart, before the driver raced off as a decoy. Iveson and Launder then took the lead, briskly walking across the track towards St. George's churchyard with the other escapees following.

"Why are they going in there?" Trenchie asked Jacob. "Do they know of a safe place to hide away?"

"I hope so, but it's as good a place as any, I suppose. Thank you, Trenchie, for rescuing us... I'll never forget what you've done."

"I heard that thou wast heading off after that lass – and thought she might be of help with the time mech... er, time box."

"Well, thanks anyway... You know, Trenchie, I'd rather die than be captured again."

"Thou may'st still die, boy, if we are found here. We would do better, I believe, by making a run for it through the fields."

With that, Trenchie unbuckled the Gallowglass's sword and gave it to Jacob. The sound of horses was now very loud and the group of escapees knelt down in the churchyard, behind the cover of the gravestones and trees. Trenchie tethered his own horse to a tree behind the church building, ready for a quick getaway if needed. To the great relief of them all, the ten-strong cavalry thundered past the church, not slowing down for an instant. Patiently and remaining quite still, they waited and listened as the sound of the horses grew quieter, until they disappeared into the night.

"We did it!" said Rachel excitedly, as she hugged each and everyone present, even the pirate. "Thanks, Trenchie... I misjudged you. There is a soft heart behind all that tough talk, isn't there?"

Trenchie felt for these people. He had heard some stories of the terrible reign of 'Bloody Mary' and wouldn't have wished upon even his worst enemy the punishments that were carried out in her name... well, perhaps. In truth, although Trenchie had been guilty of some heinous crimes in his time, he did have another side. Money was his driving force – but nevertheless, on occasion, he had been known to give away some of the proceeds of his smuggling to the most unfortunate of the poor.

Rachel looked up at the dark shape of the old yew tree, its branches an eerie silhouette against the moonlit sky. She remembered having stood in this spot on the last day she and Jacob had been together in 2011. She walked around the massive trunk, running her fingers over the bark. There seemed to be something special about a tree straddling the ages, more so than ancient monuments – it being organic.

"Imagine, Rachel, if it were that this tree could speak, what stories it would tell. Tales of times past and yet to come," Launder said, appearing like he was trying to tell Rachel something.

"Things to come? Are we not at the end?" asked Pawson, puzzled. The horrors of persecution had led Pawson to believe that the end of the world had already come, or was at least surely at the door.

"This present darkness shall lift in a measure. I cannot say unto thee of just when the end shall come," Launder went on.

As they spoke, the figures of Launder and Iveson seemed to blur, fleetingly fading into the darkness before materializing again.

"What's happening?" whispered Rachel in bewilderment. No one else understood what she meant, apart from Jacob, who had witnessed the same thing.

"This is not thy time," said Iveson.

"What are you saying?" asked Jacob confused.

Before Jacob and Rachel could enquire further, they were interrupted by the most unwelcome sound of returning horses. As the horses approached the village, Trenchie and the seven could hear that they were slowing, entering into a gentle trot until they came into view. The out-of-time fugitives could just about make out the figures of the soldiers, still mounted and busy in conversation. As they stared in the direction of their foe, they held their breath for long periods – as if even the steam they exhaled could reveal their whereabouts.

"There are only five of them; they must have split into two search parties," whispered Jacob to Trenchie, finally daring to break the silence.

"This is good, we can take 'em easy, boy."

Trenchie wriggled on his belly through the snow, closer towards the horsemen, intending a surprise attack. Taking one of the three now reloaded, single-shot pistols from his belt, he took careful aim at the nearest one.

Manasseh hastily scrambled down between the gravestones to stop him. "Friend, do not kill them for our sakes. Perchance they shall not tarry and will carry on their way."

"No, holy man, we must kill them – for otherwise they shall kill us."

"We owe thee much, my friend, but I beseech thee to shed no blood on our behalf."

"I've already shed blood on your behalf, and I shall do it again," Trenchie stubbornly retorted.

Rachel was hiding with the others further back, behind the great girth of the old yew – now a mere three and a half thousand years old, compared to the four thousand it had reached in her own time.

"Please tell me what you meant... about this not being our time," Rachel urged Iveson.

"Even to the time of the end, many shall run to and fro, and knowledge shall be increased. Go thy way, for the words are closed up and sealed till the time of the end. Many shall be purified, and made white, and tried; but the wicked shall do wickedly: and none of the wicked shall understand; but the wise shall understand."

"But I don't understand, am I wicked? Please explain it to me," she urged, though in a whisper, aware of the closeness of the soldiers.

"Thou shalt indeed understand, but go thy way – this is not thy time."

A pistol shot made Rachel jump. Trenchie's target fell to the ground, not to move again. One of the other horses reared up dismounting it's rider, whilst the remaining three rode away to regroup. Then, as if from nowhere, the other search party – who had been checking a nearby farm on foot – came running. Three had lit torches to help flush out their former captives, swords drawn in readiness. The two others had pikes, and they were soon joined by the now dismounted original group.

Trenchie was dismayed when he realized they had nine armed men to contend with, and he only had two loaded pistols. Hurriedly, he began to reload the pistol he had just used, in order to slightly increase their chances.

Manasseh, having failed to stop Trenchie's attack, dashed back up to where the others were gathered.

"Dost thou know how to use that?" Manasseh asked Jacob pointing at his sword.

"Uh... yes, I'm not bad."

"Give it unto me, before they cut thee down," Manasseh demanded.

The yeomen were in the churchyard now, and Trenchie was forced to retreat, firing off a shot that grazed one soldier – but failing to prevent his advance, sword in hand.

"Save yerselves!" yelled Trenchie, as he finished off the swordsman who was almost upon him.

Manasseh fought bravely, holding off a yeoman who had tried to capture Rachel. A pikeman then charged at him – but Trenchie, seeing this, aimed another pistol and fired. The ball of lead missed its intended target and instead hit Manasseh, who had been pushed into its path. He fell heavily to the ground and as he did so, he released his grip on the hilt of his sword, allowing it to slip through his fingers. As he lay there, he brought his arms across his chest and closed his eyes... Manasseh died – but without having to face the fire.

Trenchie now had no time to reload; instead, he grabbed the sword from the dead yeoman. After a few clashes of steel, he was forced to retreat from the advancing soldiers, until he was backed up against the old yew tree. He was surprised to see the apparently calm figures of Launder and Iveson who had remained there throughout.

In the confusion of the battle and the cover of darkness, Pawson and Pullinger were the only ones who had managed to evade capture by escaping across a field into some woodland without being seen. Rachel and Jacob had also tried to get away after Manasseh's intervention, but had been spotted and rounded up.

"Where's Reverend Manasseh?" asked Rachel, as she and Jacob were herded together with the others.

"He is dead. A better man than the one who killed him," said Trenchie, looking away.

"He is only sleeping, dear one," whispered Iveson to Rachel.

The seven surviving soldiers and their officer had them completely surrounded, and were keen to finish off the sword-wielding Trenchie.

"Shall we kill the wretch now, sir?" asked one of them of his officer.

"Wait, I wish to know from where those pistols came, first."

"How about we talk of money, lads, no man need know of yer letting us depart…" tempted the old pirate.

A couple of the soldiers showed slight expressions of interest before the officer in charge firmly quashed the idea. "We want not your money! I've lost good men tonight and how would'st thou expect me to explain that to their kin?"

Launder and Iveson stepped away from the tree and between the yeomen and Trenchie. "Take us, and leave the others," Launder pleaded with the officer.

"Thou art already in my charge and shall face trial, heretic."

Unmoved by the reply, Launder turned his head towards Rachel. As he fixed his eyes on hers he urged, "This is not thy time, go thy way."

"I don't understand," she replied, confused.

"GO THY WAY!" Launder repeated forcefully.

"Try the time mechanism, Rach," interrupted Jacob.

Rachel quickly removed the time mechanism from under the cover of her clothing. Jacob then grabbed hold of Trenchie with one hand and Rachel with the other, holding them tightly as she pressed the buttons and pulled the levers…

Chapter Ten

Polly Paine

Professor Andrew Ketterley had felt utterly horrified as his attacker vanished before his eyes. Everything he was, had and cared about had been ripped from him in an instant. All his previous excursions through time had been meticulously planned – but not this one. No money, the wrong clothes and worst of all, his nephew Jacob had no way of knowing that he was lost in time. No money, that is, but a single coin that he had found after the attack. He had been disappointed to find that it was one of his own, and just as useless in this time as having none at all.

The first night was spent sleeping rough in a barn on the outskirts of Godstone. It wasn't luxurious, but he was glad of the shelter, especially when he started to hear the sound of rain outside. As he lay down on the coarse material of some sacks he had found, he felt droplets of rainwater falling onto his face. He tried a number of locations until finally discovering a dry area. It was a far cry from Wigglesworth Road and the luxurious lifestyle to which he had grown accustomed.

It hadn't always been the way. As a child, growing up with his sister – Jacob's mother, he had been used to going without. It wasn't that they had been lacking food, but that they had always felt poor in relation to those around them. They had never been jealous, but hearing of everybody else's holidays, cars and latest gadgets had sometimes felt a bit of a drag. Things had become difficult with his dad struck by illness and having to give up his job. It had been particularly bad timing as they already had some large debts.

It was missing out on school trips, family holidays and other treats that had helped drive him to study hard and change his situation. Fortunately for him, when he and Jacob's mother were young, there hadn't been so much peer pressure concerning what you should wear, do and think.

He didn't know yet what year he was in, he hadn't had a chance to make out the date on the time mechanism when his attacker had been in possession of it. He also wondered what time the thug (Trenchie) went to, as he had not changed the dates – but he assumed that the wheels must have been knocked slightly when it fell among the bushes. He pondered over his situation for some hours, not being able to sleep, until tiredness finally won him over.

Morning brought the sound of voices and laughter outside, waking the Professor, whose back now ached from the discomfort of his 'bed'. The barn was dark except where shards of light broke through gaps in the timber cladding. Light also betrayed where the leaks of rainwater had originated. He held his breath as the voices became more distant, and he carefully pushed the door of the barn open. Unobserved, he carefully closed it again, bolting it behind him.

He was by now hungry and thirsty. There was no food in the barn and he knew that begging could soon become a realistic option. He decided that the best course of action would be to go to the Old Tree, in case Jacob came to rescue him. The worrying thing for him was that the second time mechanism was locked away in the safe. Jacob had no means of opening it – not without outside help anyway. What he was completely unaware of was the fact that his attacker and the time mechanism had somehow arrived in 2011, in his own home.

The steeple of the St. Nicholas' Church building made a good marker from which he could get his bearings. He was keen to know what year it was but decided to make no contact with the locals unless he absolutely had to. It took him over half an hour to reach the churchyard of St. George in Crowhurst, home of the ancient tree. He had spent the whole morning and much of the afternoon only vacating the area, when people came within sight. Opposite the churchyard stood a large half-brick, half-timber house. He thought he was being watched from its windows and felt rather conspicuous in his twenty-first century attire.

As afternoon headed towards evening, groups of people began to head toward the churchyard, and he took that as his cue to move on. With nowhere in particular to go, feeling very hungry and tired, he headed back towards the barn, now quite downcast.

Though hungry, he had at least been able to quench his thirst in a stream. He didn't fancy facing another day without food and realised that he couldn't take it for granted that Jacob would ever find him. He felt guilty, also for leaving his nephew in a difficult situation at home – especially after having lost both parents. There was something he wanted or, more to the point, needed to tell Jacob. He had always meant to, on some occasion, but was never sure of when would be best. Now he realised it was a secret he might have to take to the grave.

One thing that did bring a little comfort was that he had arrived in early summer. He deduced that from the kinds of plants that were in flower at the time. To have been stranded in time in the winter, especially if he was in the 'Little Ice Age', would have been a bitter state of affairs. He made the walk back through the countryside that was as beautiful as ever.

However, when you have worries, as he certainly did, it's hard to appreciate such things.

It wasn't the walking or even the lack of food that made him feel tired. Distressing thoughts that he may have lost everything he held dear, even his own identity, seemed to drain his energy away. In normal circumstances, he would have considered any obstacle just a challenge to be overcome, but these circumstances seemed overwhelmingly bleak.

Inside the partially rotting shelter of the barn, he again arranged the old sacks into a makeshift bed. It was barely evening when he curled up and tried to focus his mind on what he should do next. He came to the decision that he would again make the journey to the Old Tree, in the hope that Jacob somehow would find him. He realised that he could easily have found a barn nearer the old tree to sleep in – however, all the stress had confused his normally logical decision-making.

Night passed and Jacob's uncle slept soundly this time, but the early morning found him being tentatively prodded by the boot of a labourer.

"Wake up!" urged the middle-aged man, as his wife looked on, concerned.

"Careful now, Andrew, he is most likely a drunkard and could be a danger."

Andrew Knox was wary of the unusually dressed man, who was now sitting upright. Anticipating the stranger's reaction, he held tightly to the handle of his spade – just in case he might need a weapon.

"What art thou doing here, stranger?" questioned Mrs Knox.

"I just wanted a place to rest, I'm sorry if I have trespassed… I'll go now." As the Professor rose to his feet, he felt the labourer's firm grip upon his shoulder.

"Stranger, thou seemest not to be a drunkard and thy manner is quite refined. Even thy clothes are most unlike any

I have seen. Where be thou from, sir?" Mrs Knox asked, her voice softening.

"My name is Andrew Ketterley, I'm from…" The Professor stopped himself from saying more, fearing that his story could bring an accusation of witchcraft.

"I am called Andrew also… Andrew Knox and this is my wife Clare," said the labourer as he released his grip. "Hast thou eaten? If not, come eat with us, and tell us thy story. I believe thou hast much to tell."

The couple seemed friendly enough, their initial apprehension at finding a stranger in the barn being understandable. The offer of food was something the Professor couldn't refuse and he appreciated their act of kindness, but was surprised by their trust. They walked about half a mile through a copse of trees and past a field to a tiny thatched cottage where the Knox family lived.

Inside, a little girl played on the dirt floor with a pile of small stones. She would raise them up above her head and then drop them onto a metal plate, enjoying the clattering sounds as they fell.

"This is our daughter, Charlotte," said Mrs Knox as she swept the infant up into her arms.

"She's lovely," complimented the Professor.

"Dost thou have children, Mr Ketterley?"

"I remember that I have a nephew called Jacob, but my memory is rather clouded, I'm afraid. You see, I was attacked by a robber and barely can remember anything – not even where I'm from," he lied to conceal his real story.

"Thou poor soul, please accept our hospitality until you are well. We have not much, but we are happy to share," Mrs Knox offered charitably.

The Professor felt very moved by her generosity, especially in the light of their obvious poverty. Mr Knox lit the fire, fanning the flames until they flickered around a kettle containing some soup his wife had made the previous day.

"May I ask you, Mr and Mrs Knox, what year are we in?" asked the Professor as he finished the small bowl of soup.

"Well, of course it be 1687, sir. Surely the vagabond who assailed you has done a terrible thing to your mind," answered the visibly shocked Andrew Knox.

"He did, Mr Knox, but there are only certain things I can't remember. I'm sure I will be better soon," reassured the Professor.

Once they had all finished, they rose from the table and the coin that had edged its way to the opening of the Professor's trouser pocket slipped onto the floor. Mrs Knox spotted it first and stooped to pick it up before Charlotte could get to it. She assumed that it must be some foreign currency, as it was different to their coinage. She was quite bewildered when she read the date of 2011 and saw the image of Queen Elizabeth the Second.

"Andrew, may I speak with thee about a matter?"

The Professor thought she meant him for a moment, until he saw Andrew Knox step outside the front door with his wife. He thought nothing of it, until they returned looking quite stern.

"Mr Ketterley, be there a matter that thou art deliberately concealing from us?" questioned Mr Knox, as he held the fifty pence coin up for the Professor to see.

"I found it..."

"Didst thou also find thine unusual clothing, sir, and why is it that thou speak'st in a different manner to us? Even the Evelyn family and other educated folk speak not like you," said Mrs Knox, looking hurt by this apparent deception.

"There is someone thou must see," added Mr Knox.

"I'm not a witch..." insisted the Professor, starting to panic.

The couple reassured Jacob's uncle of their good intent and with Charlotte being carried in Mr Knox's arms; they set off towards the building of St. Nicholas' Church. They told him of the Reverend Butts, who they believed would understand and be of help.

"We were preparing to go to the morning service when I saw thee lying in the barn. I did not wait for a second, but ran home with much haste to warn my husband," explained Mrs Knox, "Reverend Butts will no doubt be wondering at our absence."

The Professor felt firmly unconvinced that this 'Reverend Butts' would be of much help, and was wary of saying anything incriminating.

Inside the building, he wandered around – impressed by the architecture. He stopped to read the list of rectors who had held that office over the years. James Manasseh was one of those mentioned, but the name held no significance for him.

"Good day, sir, I believe I have not yet made thine acquaintance," came the greeting from an elderly looking man, entering the sanctuary through the door of the vestry.

"No, we haven't met," answered the Professor.

"Reverend Butts," started Mrs Knox, "we were hoping that thou may'st be able to help our friend, Mr Ketterley. He is a stranger here and cannot remember much at all, that after a villain attacked him."

"Yes, sir, and our friend also came upon this mysterious coin," Mr Knox said as he handed it to the cleric.

The aged Reverend Butts with his mop of curly grey hair gazed intently at the fifty pence coin, so unlike any he had seen – well, except for one other.

"Tell me, Mr Knox, who else knows of this matter?" asked Reverend Butts.

"Only us, sir."

Reverend Butts walked down one of the aisles to the doors and bolted them — just as one of his predecessors had when Jacob had been the out-of-time stranger.

"Please follow me," Reverend Butts urged, as he headed back to the vestry.

Once inside, the rector, with the help of Mr Knox, slid a heavy oak chest across the floor to reveal a wooden cover that hid the steps into a cellar. Mrs Knox handed Reverend Butts a candle, which he took down with him into the damp space beneath. He brushed the cobwebs from his face as he made his way down the narrow steps. The cellar had become something of a home for items that might one day become useful — or perhaps 'junk' was a more apt description.

Moving some woodworm-infested pieces of timber to one side, Reverend Butts found what he was looking for — a bundle of mould-stained cloth.

"Mr Ketterley, perhaps these unusual artefacts will aid thy memory," suggested the cleric as he lay the dusty bundle onto a table, back up in the vestry.

"What are they?" muttered the Professor.

"I was of the hope that thou may'st be the one to enlighten us," came Reverend Butts' reply.

Mr Knox carefully unwrapped the cloth as if something precious was hid within. The Professor was astonished to see a mobile phone, battery torch, lipstick, and an assortment of coins unveiled before him.

"Hast thou ever seen the likes of these, Mr Ketterley?" asked Mrs Knox.

"Where did you find them?" queried the Professor as he examined the mobile phone.

"They were found in the possession of a woman by the name of Polly Paine... a hundred years ago and more. There had been rumours that she was involved in witchcraft, even before the discovery, but that was dismissed as the chatter of drunkards. However, one day, a man of good repute and loyal servant of the Evelyn family saw her with the very item that thou holdest in thy hand now. It was reported to make the strangest of noises."

Reverend Butts frowned as he continued the story: "Sadly, this roused a mob who accused her of sorcery and blamed her for the poor harvest that year. She claimed to have accidentally happened upon these unfathomable objects and denied knowledge of them. The mysterious thing is that the artefact that thou hast there, has never made a noise since then."

The Professor was really excited at the find, but showed no emotion. He was still afraid that if he acknowledged his connection to the future, he could be accused of witchcraft and the tale of Polly Paine only increased that fear.

"My memory is still quite cloudy – I don't know what these objects are," claimed the Professor.

"That is indeed a pity, sir," declared Mr Knox with obvious disappointment. "The coin thou didst find is identical to one of these others. We think not that Polly Paine was a witch; but that she told the truth when she confessed to finding them. Perhaps when thy mind becomes sound, thou wilt provide us with the answer to this mystery."

The cleric and Mr and Mrs Knox looked intently at the Professor, as if waiting for him to confess all, but he kept his silence.

"Thank you, Mr Ketterley, for coming here this day. It is, I believe, time to bring these matters to a conclusion – that of thy memory loss and of the origin of these items. There is one man in this land who may offer us explanation. Would'st thou like to join me in travelling to Cambridge to meet him? His name is Newton... Isaac Newton."

The Professor was more than aware of who Isaac Newton was. By the end of Newton's life, his accumulated achievements would establish him as perhaps the greatest scientist of all time. "I think I do recall the name," he answered, rubbing his head as if to feign memory loss.

Despite being less than convinced by Professor Ketterley's story, Mr and Mrs Knox generously agreed to allow Professor Ketterley to stay with them – until it was time for him to make his journey to Cambridge. Newton was known for his mood swings; they hoped that the Professor would catch him on a good day.

Sunday was the only day off work for the majority of the people, and early Monday brought a return to their hard existence. Mr Knox spent six days a week working on the Evelyn family estate. The Evelyns were wealthy landowners and had some ancestral links to the French 'Evelin' family, who had been heavily involved in the crusades and intermarried with the royal families of Jerusalem and Cyprus.

Life was hard for Mr Knox, working long hours in all weathers. His duties varied from maintenance of the barns and other outbuildings to milking cows, harvesting crops and just about anything where another pair of hands was needed. With their agricultural lifestyle, all depended on what the times and seasons demanded.

Though his work was hard, Andrew Knox was quite content. He had known no other way of life, and it seemed a better thing to him to be poor in the country than be poor in the towns and cities. Here, at least he could enjoy the beauty of the woods and fields with the sun on his back – well, now and again anyway. Just to eat and spend a bit of time with his family in the evening was enough after a hard day, and it made Sunday's rest even more precious.

Monday's first task was to repair the leaky barn that had been the Professor's shelter during his first two nights in 1687. Professor Ketterley went with him, thinking it was the least he could do to lend a hand. Jacob's uncle found it hard to keep up with his host as he went about his day's work with almost no break. He was filled with admiration for Andrew Knox and felt slightly embarrassed at his lack of fitness and skills in the tasks set before them. The labourer recognised that the Professor was unaccustomed to manual work, his soft hands being a giveaway, but made no mention of the fact.

Back in the Knox family's tiny home, the Professor enjoyed the rather basic meal offered to him with a gratitude he had never felt before. He wished that he had some money with him to repay their generosity, but thought that perhaps it was the little they had that brought out the best in them. Still, he would have been happier if they weren't quite so poor.

The next few days continued in the same manner, his body increasingly aching as he worked it harder than at any time since his youth. While the Professor learnt a new way of life, Reverend Butts wrote to Cambridge University, the home of Isaac Newton, to request a visit. The correspondence would take a number of days, as he had to wait for the mail coach to deliver his letter and bring back the reply.

After one particularly hard day, which had involved a great deal of digging, the Professor decided he needed a day's rest as he was beginning to suffer from back pain. Mr Knox graciously agreed and besides, he had never insisted that his guest should come and work to earn his keep.

The Professor spent the following day wandering through the countryside. He appreciated the beauty of the landscape more now, having made some friends and with at least a temporary place to stay. He reasoned that if worse came to worse, he could at least earn a living as a labourer. However, at forty-seven and having had a rather sedentary lifestyle, he had doubts as to whether his body could stand up to it, especially when the harsher winters of this time period would strike.

Chapter Eleven

Observations

The Professor walked towards the site of a water mill previously used for making gunpowder, but no longer in existence in the modern day. Fields and hedges reigned in places where houses would later stand. The sun mostly succeeded in penetrating the blanket of clouds, and a strong breeze was blowing, causing the trees and bushes to shake and the leaves above his head to rustle.

Leigh Mill was owned by the Evelyn family and again now grinding corn to feed mouths rather than gunpowder for taking lives. As he got nearer, he could see people going into the mill with linen bags to get some flour, as the paddles of the wheel cut through the water of the pond that serviced it.

Stopping by the edge of the pond on the far side of the mill, he watched as a moorhen led her young through the bulrushes along the water's edge. He remained there for a time, observing the coots, reed warblers and various other birds that had made their home there.

He could still feel slight pain in his back and neck, but was glad to have taken a rest from physical activity before it became any worse. It was while walking away from the pond amongst bushes and sweet-smelling chestnut trees, that another pain was inflicted.

A man leapt upon him from behind the cover of the bushes,

dragging him to the ground. A second man, older than the first, kicked him hard in the chest. The Professor curled up on the ground trying to regain breath, as the younger of the two assailants rose to his feet and drew a pistol from his belt.

"That is him for sure. He be the one I saw with Trenchie before he disappeared," said the younger man to the older.

"I don't know what you want... are you the one who took the little wooden box from me?" the Professor asked the older man. The older man was not dissimilar in build and looks to his original attacker (Trenchie) and could easily be mistaken for him.

The younger man went to kick him again, but the older one stopped him, gesturing with his hand. "It is I who will ask the questions. Is it true that thou know'st of the whereabouts of Trenchman? Davy here says he saw thee together with him, the last time he was seen."

"There was a man who robbed me, he took something of mine and then he went away," answered the Professor, not wishing to explain just how he went.

"I reckon he informed the law, let me shoot 'im, Collie," urged the vicious subordinate.

"Rumour around here has it that he has lost his memory. Now if that be true and I deem that most unlikely, we had better let him live – for now," replied 'Collie', who was the second in command of Trenchie's gang and had just released from gaol.

Jacob's uncle once again felt his heart pounding fast as Collie addressed him: "Listen to me carefully, speak of this meeting and we will take thy life, along with those that thou art staying with. Dost thou understand?"

The Professor demonstrated his compliance with a nod and the two were soon out of his sight, disappearing through the trees and leaving him a forlorn figure on the ground. Once again left clutching bruised ribs, he raised himself onto his knees before getting fully to his feet. The pleasantness of his country walk had turned into something much darker – and rather than continue further, he headed back towards the little cottage. He pondered whether or not to tell his hosts of his encounter, but decided it would perhaps be wise not to.

That evening, the Professor wasn't very talkative, his mind mulling over the events of the day. The world of 1687, which had seemed less daunting since meeting Reverend Butts and the Knox family, had revealed its sinister side. When he had been attacked on arrival, and his time mechanism had been stolen, he thought at least he had seen the last of the thug. Now, it was clear that the original attacker was not alone – and that he had a gang of criminals to deal with.

Professor Ketterley had almost lost his appetite, but that didn't stop him from finishing the plate of pottage, which wasn't very large. "Come on, Jake, find me…" he muttered to himself, as he stepped outside the cottage gazing up at the stars. Lowering his gaze back down to the view of the fields in front of the cottage, he caught sight of what looked like a rider in the distance. The figure grew larger as it seemed to be heading in their direction. The Professor watched anxiously, remembering the threats he had heard earlier, and wondered again whether to warn Mr and Mrs Knox.

Andrew Knox joined him outside. Noticing his guest gazing towards the far edge of the field, he turned his head in that direction also. "It be Reverend Butts most likely, perhaps he has received a reply, Mr Ketterley."

On hearing that, the Professor relaxed somewhat and then eagerly watched as the horseman drew ever closer. It soon became clear that Mr Knox was correct – it was indeed Reverend Butts.

"Good news, Mr Ketterley," announced the cleric as he dismounted.

"Do you mean this... Isaac Newton will see me?" enquired the Professor, still trying to put on the memory loss act.

"He will, sir, and we shall set for Cambridge tomorrow morn. I have taken the liberty of arranging for a stagecoach to come for us then. I know the driver well, he has taken me there before and has agreed to meet us outside the church." "Well done, sir, now wilt thou come in and sup with us?" asked Mrs Knox.

"Thank you, Mrs Knox, I would be happy to. I have brought you a gift as well, although it is surely too late in the day, to cook it now."

Mrs Knox was delighted to see that Reverend Butts had brought them a whole chicken, a rare treat for them.

Reverend Butts had struck up a very good friendship with Andrew and Clare Knox over the years. He enjoyed their company and was as happy to dine with them as he would have been with any Lord or Lady. He had also spent time teaching them to read and would often lend them books from his personal library.

"Mr Ketterley, put not all thy hope in Mr Newton. Most likely, thy memory will return soon anyway. To be struck on the head can do terrible things to one's mind. Nevertheless, I am sure thou shalt see recovery," assured Reverend Butts, finishing the last of the pottage.

Bidding them good night, Reverend Butts requested that the Professor be at the St. Nicholas' Church building by ten o'clock in the morning. He was going to ask him to travel light, but clearly, that was not going to be necessary.

The Professor had grown accustomed to going to bed early. There was no television, radio or anything else to keep him or the Knox family up late – and besides, why waste unnecessary money on candles when you're tired from the day's exertions. Morning light was the signal for a new day's work to begin. Mr Knox wished the Professor a safe journey to Cambridge before he set off to fulfil his own tasks.

It had rained the previous night, and drops of rain were still falling from the tips of leaves as the wind blew. The Professor was still wearing the same clothes as when he had first arrived in 1687. He had managed to wash them, and he did have a spare set of rather tatty clothing that Andrew Knox had found for him – probably from someone no longer in need of them. Arriving a little early at the village of Godstone, he paused for a while at an inn named the 'Bell'. As time neared for the start of the journey, he made the short walk to the church building of St. Nicholas.

He could see that the stagecoach was just arriving as he approached the church building. It looked rather old, well worn, and was drawn by four brown horses. Its wheels were painted bright red, and the side panels and roof of the U-shaped compartment were a pale blue.

Reverend Butts left the building through the door of the vestry and saw Professor Ketterley waiting inside the lychgate. "Good morning, sir. Mr Kent kindly agreed to stop here for us, but we must not keep him waiting," he said as he nodded towards the driver.

The driver busied himself loading up Reverend Butts' luggage, which was already in a pile by the roadside. The Professor opened the door of the carriage and climbed inside. The cracked brown leather seats, facing each other, offered space for four people, but it had been arranged that no other passengers would be joining them. The Reverend and Jacob's uncle both opted to share the rear seat in order to be facing forward during what would be quite a long journey.

It wasn't long before the Professor began to wish he was back in his 'Flying Spur'. The roads were generally in a wretched state, making for an uncomfortable and painfully slow trip. The scenery was pleasant enough, although not particularly varied, and he had to concede it was at least easier than working with Mr Knox. They stopped at various coach houses along the way in order to change horses. Sometimes they also stopped for pre-arranged meetings with friends of Reverend Butts'. The final stop for the day was in a small town called Hoddesdon. It was there that they would spend the night rather than continue towards Cambridge, desiring to feel refreshed when they met Newton.

The driver brought his team of horses to a halt in the high street of Hoddesdon, the Professor glad to see the end of the day's bumpy journey. In the centre of the town, a line of people could be seen queuing up before the stone statue of a woman holding a large jug. From the jug poured the town's public water supply, piped from a point about half a mile away.

"We call the statue the 'Samaritan Woman', sir," commented the driver to Reverend Butts.

"Aptly named, Mr Kent," he replied as they joined the back of the queue.

The people in front were a mixture of locals and other travellers. A young woman at the front filled a bucket to the brim to take back to her house. They waited patiently until it was their turn to drink and then splattered the cool liquid over their faces, after what had been a warm day. Once refreshed, Mr Kent drove the stagecoach away, leaving Reverend Butts and the Professor to find themselves a place to stay for the night.

After a quick look around they settled for an inn called the 'Bull' as their place of rest. It was opposite a building called the 'market house'; the two buildings were connected at first floor level by a wood beam that sported a sign for the inn.

The Professor felt slightly embarrassed as Reverend Butts paid the landlord for the rent of a couple of rooms for the night. He had never been the sort to 'sponge' off others, but he had no choice but to accept any kind offer he was given.

The inn seemed to be almost full. The town itself benefited much from travellers stopping there, mostly those also making the journey between London and Cambridge. The inn wasn't, as the Professor feared, full of drunks, but in fact quite restrained. Seating was scarce but he managed to find an empty bench in a corner of the spacious room. A man in his twenties was sitting at the table there writing, but he seemed happy for the Professor to join him there.

Professor Ketterley felt rather awkward, as the rather studious young man would, from time to time, stop from his work to cast a suspicious glance.

"Sir, if I may be so bold... thy clothing, it is most uncommon. Something tells me thou hast a story well worth the telling," the man suggested.

"Well... I may or may not, but why do you want to know?" snapped the Professor, feeling a little irritated by the apparent nosiness of the stranger.

"Forgive me, sir, I should make it known to you that I am a writer and have an interest in anything that flies away from the ordinary. Let me introduce myself, my name is Matthew Prior."

The Professor resisted a smile when he realised that he was talking to someone who was to become a well-known poet, among other things. "Professor Andrew Ketterley, pleased to meet you," he declared.

From then on, the Professor proceeded to tease the young writer with hints of having a remarkable story to tell but never revealing enough detail. He was actually desperate to tell of his secret, especially to someone of good intellect – but Prior wasn't to be the one.

They were soon joined by Reverend Butts who had bought some meat pies for their evening meal. When the Professor had finished his largest meal since arriving in 1687, they left the table and went to their rooms. Prior the poet sat in silence and considered his conversation with the strangely dressed 'Professor' before ripping up his notes, leaving them discarded on the table, as he left the inn.

They were met with a shower of hailstones the following morning as they left the door of the 'Bull'. Mr Kent and the stagecoach were waiting outside for them, and they rushed to get inside it. As they journeyed north along the rutted roads, the weather began to improve. The grey clouds that had greeted them were gradually replaced with a scattering of fluffy white ones.

Travelling by stagecoach had been a novelty for about the first thirty minutes after leaving Godstone. However, the combination of the bumpy surface and interminably slow rate of travel had soon dispelled that. The one saving grace for Professor Ketterley was that he was getting closer to the world's greatest thinker – certainly of that time. The stagecoach stopped for the penultimate time before Cambridge in a place called 'Buntingford'. Another timber-framed coaching inn gave them the opportunity to rest – not the 'Bull' this time, but the 'Black Bull'. Their last stop on the way was at a flint-built coach house near Royston, appropriately called the 'Coach and Horses'.

The Professor was by now aching to reach Cambridge and put an end to the uncomfortable ride, apart from anything else. He was glad that the final stop was a brief one, even though it meant having to take to his hard leather seat again so quickly. The driver set the team of horses in motion, surprised at the unusually dressed passenger's claims of discomfort. He was very proud of the vehicle, considering it to be quite splendid.

Jacob's uncle gazed out of the window across the seemingly endless countryside as the coach headed towards the university town. He pondered over how little difference there was between here in 1687 and many of the other time-periods he had visited. Transport had been reliant on horses for thousands of years, and rural life wasn't greatly different for the average person, whether they had been born in 1200 AD or 1700 AD. The contrast was so stark with the Professor's own time, where nothing seemed to stand still for long – technology increased at such a rate that the latest innovations soon became outdated; even attitudes and principles changed as quickly as the seasons.

The countryside around Cambridge was quite marshy; willow trees seemed particularly abundant. Entering the town, the Professor was slightly disappointed by the disrepair of some of the buildings. The paving was quite uneven and the medieval streets typically narrow. The road widened as it reached into the marketplace which bustled with people buying and selling their wares. Pies appeared to be the 17th century equivalent of take-away food, reminding the Professor of the many old nursery rhymes that gave them mention.

From the market, the stagecoach turned right into Trinity Street. Mr Kent looked ahead at the extravagant sight of the castle-like 'Great Gate' as the entrance to Trinity College came into view. The Great Gate was a huge gatehouse, each corner guarded by a turreted tower. There were two doors in the tower; one large, the other small. In a niche above them stood a statue of the college's founder – Henry VIII.

Mr Kent brought the coach to a halt and entered the imposing gatehouse to explain the reason for their visit. Whilst he was doing so, the Professor and Reverend Butts stepped down from the carriage to stretch their legs and admire the architecture.

"A truly awe inspiring sight, Mr Ketterley," said Reverend Butts in admiration.

It was. They could see beyond the large entrance into the Great Court of the college, the largest court on the university grounds. As they looked, two of the college staff came to collect the luggage from the stagecoach. Once they had thanked Mr Kent for his work, they made their way through the large entrance. It was by now five o'clock, as was revealed to them by the clock on the tower to the west of the large arched-windowed chapel. Students were milling around the court as well. One was washing himself in the fountain in the centre, a detailed construction with Greek-style pillars, arches and ornate roof.

"Reverend Butts, welcome to Trinity," greeted them an elegantly-dressed man wearing a long black wig.

"Thank you, sir, but the pleasure is ours indeed," he replied.

"Professor Newton is expecting you, gentlemen. He is to be found reading in Nevile's Court."

They were led up some stone steps into a large hall and then through it into another courtyard, this one surrounded by cloisters on three sides. This court was smaller, but still beautifully designed. Opposite them, on the other side of the court, stood the new library designed by Wren, but as yet not completed.

Alone, absorbed by a book he was reading, sat a middle-aged man, his white shirt unbuttoned at the top as a concession to the summer. He seemed unaware of their presence at first, and that of the other people who passed by him. Their guide walked over to where the man sat in the shade of the cloisters, gesturing to the two visitors to follow before leaving them alone and walking back up the steps into the huge hall.

"I trust that the journey was a pleasant one, gentlemen. Thou must be Mr Ketterley, my dear friend Reverend Butts has enlightened me of thy situation," the great scientist remarked to Jacob's uncle.

Professor Ketterley felt quite 'star-struck', as a fan might, when meeting a famous movie actor or actress – but more so. He was surprised at the small stature of Newton, average perhaps for his time, but smaller than the statues of him that the Professor had seen in his own time. Newton's hair was shorter than the Professor imagined it would be, as he wasn't wearing the sort of long wig he sometimes would in portraits. The three men sat down together, on Newton's invitation, with the Professor feeling uncharacteristically nervous.

"It's really wonderful to meet you, Sir Isaac," he mumbled.

Newton looked at him quizzically, as he hadn't even been knighted at this stage. "You flatter me sir, but just Professor Newton or Mr Newton will suffice," he suggested without the hint of a smile.

"I must confess Mr Ketterley, there was another reason I suggested this meeting. Thou seest sir, thou art not the first 'time sojourner' to cross our path," stated Reverend Butts.

"I don't know what you mean!" protested Professor Ketterley.

"Come now sir; the unusual accent, a use of our language neither proper nor common, clothing of a design and manufacture so different and a coin dated centuries in the future. What other explanation can be offered? Perchance, a rogue did inflict such an injury that caused thy memory to fail. Perchance also that he dressed thee in this manner and put the coin into thy pocket whilst thou wast asleep. All things are possible, but this seems most unlikely indeed," declared Reverend Butts, sounding a bit like a detective.

Newton remained quiet, focussing on Professor Ketterley's body language. He had also observed that the clothing the Professor wore, though by no means unusual in terms of colour or extravagance (he was wearing a white shirt, black trousers and black laced shoes), did not belong in their time. It was clear to him that there was something so different about the type of material, stitching, and style that it couldn't be explained by the individualism of a particular tailor.

Professor Ketterley felt like he had been painted into a corner with nowhere to go. His impression of an innocent who was suffering from memory loss had seemed a little desperate from the beginning. To continue it now seemed rather futile. "This is very difficult for me, and I am willing to tell you more – but first, please tell me what you know. What do you mean by 'not the first time sojourner'? Have you seen a young man called Jacob? He's my nephew... has he come looking for me?" his questions flowed.

"Mr Ketterley, we have encountered only one other individual whom we termed a 'time sojourner'. It was not a young man, but a maid – and not of this nation. She was exceedingly afraid at first; she would say nothing until we managed to gain her trust," explained Reverend Butts.

"What did she look like, and how did you find her?" asked Professor Ketterley, keen to know more.

"It was in February of the year past that she appeared. I was alone in the building of St. Nicholas' in Godstone when I heard the sound of footsteps running down an aisle. I walked towards the noise, with a candle to guide me. The building was lit, but only dimly. Then, on hearing noises near the entrance, I called out, but no answer came. In front of the doors, I found this young maid of about fourteen or fifteen years, in a state of panic. I was startled by the fact that she was from a nation far away, most likely African by her skin tone. I have met very few foreigners in Godstone, probably only a handful passing through and they from no further than France and the surrounding nations," Reverend Butts elaborated.

"What happened to her?" asked the Professor.

"My wife came and together we managed to calm the maid and take her to our home. The people of the village took great delight in her, especially the children, whom she taught new games of which they had never seen the like. Though she smiled and laughed with the children, I did not feel at ease. She spoke not one word of English and we knew not where she was from, nor anything of her family. I have known Professor Newton no short while, and it was to him that I turned for help. The journey we have made this day was the same as that I made with Esti," Reverend Butts concluded.

"Dost thou know of that name?" Newton asked as he observed the reaction of Jacob's uncle.

Professor Ketterley slowly shook his head and Newton continued: "I perceived that the maid was in fact acquainted with our language, or at least of a language derived from it. She showed signs of recognition of our words at times, but an ability to converse in English, she demonstrated not. With some difficulties, I did manage to communicate in a Semitic language close to her own. Slowly, but with increasing success, we made certain of her story, a most fantastical story that would to most be incredulous."

Isaac Newton then recounted the details of the encounter: The girl's name was Esti Falasha-Mura, a subject of the land of Abyssinia (which the Professor recognised as modern day Ethiopia). She had amazed them by her claim that she was from 1995 – a revelation that seemed to shake Jacob's uncle to the core. Disturbingly for Newton and Reverend Butts, Esti had also vividly described a threatening group of people who were seeking her. It was by means of an old, small wooden box, of which there were seven in total, that she had somehow been translated through time and escaped.

"With the utmost respect, Professor Newton – why would you accept such an account with no evidence?" asked Professor Ketterley. It was easy now for Jacob's uncle to believe this type of story, but he couldn't understand how Newton could accept such a tale, never having experienced time travel.

"Dear Mr Ketterley, I would not countenance such a story if there were nothing to corroborate it. I have witnessed with my own eyes the artefacts from the future that remain in Reverend Butts' possession. Esti also bore testimony to such advance of knowledge and travel; I could only be reminded of the words of Daniel: *'Seal the book, even to the time of the end: many shall run to and fro, and knowledge shall be increased'."*

"Where is she now?" asked Professor Ketterley.

"It is to our deep regret that we know not the answer to that question. Esti and I returned to Godstone where she stayed with my wife and me. It was on the sixth day from arriving back home, that we heard screams coming from Esti's room. We entered it without hesitation, only to find it empty and with the window still closed," answered Reverend Butts.

"And the little wooden box?"

"She called it a 'Kairos Box' – it too had gone. Professor Newton was keen to see it as Esti had left it in Godstone when we came here to see him. I had already agreed to make another journey to Cambridge with Esti and the box, but the opportunity was denied us," Reverend Butts continued.

"It must be clear now, Mr Ketterley, why Reverend Butts desired that you journeyed here. If 'twas that thou wast suffering from memory loss, it would not be my help that thou would'st need. It is not that we seek knowledge of things beyond our time – in fact, I would that talk of such things should cease now... they are not for us. No, our desire is to know if we can help Esti and why 'time sojourners' are manifesting in the village of Godstone," stated Newton, looking into the Professor's eyes. "However, sirs, as much as I long to know more, I must confess to having been a poor host. Let us dine first and then renew our conversation."

Isaac Newton spoke with the staff in the dining hall, before leading the two men back into the aptly named Great Court. They walked to the building that bridged the chapel and the Great Gate. Newton led them up a staircase to the first floor where his rooms were situated. It was here that Newton wrote some of his greatest work – work that would define him as arguably the most influential scientist of all time.

Professor Ketterley and Reverend Butts made themselves comfortable in a considerably large wood panelled room. It was illuminated by a brass chandelier with eight tall candles which Newton had just ignited. There were upholstered chairs made of walnut – and even a couple of armchairs, which were just coming into vogue, for those who could afford them. From the rear windows, they could look upon Newton's own private garden, which could be accessed by a covered staircase. Isaac liked to spend time alone in the garden, a place of solitude to think and to imagine. He had incredible energy and concentration, but everyone needs rest – and the garden offered him that place when the weather allowed.

Jacob's uncle sat down in one of the crimson armchairs, the sort you might see on display in a stately home. Here, however, they held their vivid colour that had not faded, nor was the material worn by time. He felt quite sleepy – not that he'd done much, but the long, slow journey had left him tired. It wasn't just the travelling; the worry of his predicament had made it difficult for him to sleep properly. Since arriving in 1687, he had spent most nights lying awake, as he tried to come up with ideas how to make the best of the situation. Here in Cambridge, he felt that he had people with whom he could unburden himself – and that was an immense relief.

Newton was readying the dining room with some of the college staff who had brought with them the food he had requested from the college dining hall. Once everything was to his satisfaction, the staff left and he opened the doors that divided him from his guests. "Gentlemen, welcome to my table – I hope the food will be to your satisfaction."

The Professor was in no doubt that it would be. Much as he appreciated Mrs Knox's cooking, the portions were never quite enough. She also didn't have the food budget of Trinity College,

Cambridge to call upon. Following a prayer of thanksgiving, they began with soup, to his initial disappointment – he'd had rather a lot of soup recently. However, this was followed by roast duck and an assortment of vegetables as well as pastries, a meal that seemed to him the finest he'd ever had.

Their conversation during the meal was pleasant enough, but not particularly profound. Once the course was finished, they enjoyed some fruit tarts and then cleared the table, keeping only some port and cheese to indulge in as their talk returned to the subject of time.

"Mr Ketterley, earlier when we spoke in the court, thou gavest mention that thou hast more to tell. Please be at ease, sir – thy words from the three of us shall pass not. It is also assured that the details recounted by Esti Falasha-Mura shall remain between Reverend Butts, his dear lady wife, thyself and me," affirmed Newton.

"Professor Newton is absolutely right – thou hast nothing to fear from us," reassured Reverend Butts.

"Thank you, I do trust you – and frankly it's a relief to be able to talk about this. My name genuinely is Andrew Ketterley. I am a Professor also, and you are right – I am not from your time. I was born in 1964 and I left my time-period in 2011. I was given one of those little wooden boxes, which I call 'time mechanisms'," he began.

Isaac Newton leaned forward as Jacob's uncle mentioned the boxes. He was torn between the thirst for knowledge and an instinctive feeling that not all details of the future were meant for them. His fascination had led him to learn a lot of information about the future from Esti, perhaps too much. In the time that had elapsed since then, he and Reverend Butts had decided to reject and try to forget that which they had learned, to dismiss it as fable.

"Professor Ketterley, our time is not ready for all that thou could'st speak of. There are things that must take place, some good and some bad. Before thou speak'st forth, may I ask that thou sparest us details of invention and events of history that bear no relation to thy story or that of Esti," requested Newton.

"Certainly. Well, I can tell you that the boxes are not the invention of my time-period. They are old as if from the ancient past, and yet they operate with a power that defies logic. I tried to operate them – I actually had two –, many times without effect. Then, on one occasion, as I examined the object – it just happened. I was translated through time. From that instance, every time I tried to use it, it worked perfectly. I knew that there was nothing about the box in a physical sense that could explain its power. After many successful journeys in time, I trusted it enough to take my only living relative with me," explained Professor Ketterley.

"May I know what became of thy 'time mechanisms'?" asked Reverend Butts.

"One was stolen by the robber, the other remains in 2011."

"And Esti – dost thou know of her?" enquired Newton.

"I don't know her, but I do know of her. She was helping my sister and her husband on a project they were working on in Ethiopia, what you call Abyssinia. They had been missing for about fifteen years when I left my time period. I don't know anything about the people you say were after her – but it frightens me, to be honest. I'm worried that they have something to do with my sister's disappearance."

Jacob's uncle and Reverend Butts spent the next three days in Cambridge. The professor was overjoyed at being allowed to witness Newton at work, although he was constantly reminded not to give away any information about scientific discoveries beyond the famous scientist's own time.

In one of Newton's workrooms stood an old oak table; upon it stood a scale model of the solar system. "That's a beautiful piece of work, Professor Newton," remarked Jacob's uncle as he operated a crank that made the various globes rotate and orbit.

"Thank you, though I must confess that it is not my craftsmanship. What is strange is that some who admire the design in this small imitation cannot see any design in that which it is modelled upon," commented Newton.

"Professor Newton, may I ask what you consider your greatest achievements – so far," asked Professor Ketterley.

"Anything I have achieved has been built on the work of my predecessors."

"As if standing on the shoulders of giants?" suggested Professor Ketterley.

"Thou hast the tongue of a poet! My most important work is yet not complete, a book…"

"'Principia'?" anticipated Professor Ketterley.

"No, 'Principia' is complete and recently published. It shall be called: 'Observations on the Prophecies of Daniel and the Apocalypse of St. John'," declared Newton.

"Well… it's a catchy title!" joked Professor Ketterley. It was a joke that went down like a lead balloon, and he realised that the 17th century wasn't ready for his ironic humour just yet.

Chapter Twelve

Forgotten Words
and Binds that Tie

A cannonball ripped through the rough sawn timbers of the nearby barn, to the cries of those within. Musket shots followed as the 'Roundheads' made their advance.

"Get down!" shouted Jacob, pulling Rachel to the ground.

Trenchie had been the first to dive for cover, his instinct for survival having spared him from many a brush with death over the years.

Another cannonball whizzed over their heads and through the branches of the Old Tree, scattering splinters of wood and bark. The mighty frame of the old yew stood firm in its wake, adding yet another story to its long life. The outnumbered group of royalist 'Cavaliers' continued their defiant stand, in and around the barn, only about two hundred metres from where the three were lying – but they were heavily outgunned.

As stray gunfire pitted the area around them, Jacob and Rachel hurriedly tried to reset their time mechanisms, which had inexplicably taken them to the year 1643 and into the midst of the English Civil War. Some of the musket shots now seemed to be aimed directly at them as they lay prostrate on the ground – either or both sides thinking them to be enemy combatants.

"What the hell is Trenchie doing!" gasped Jacob, as the old pirate began to make his way towards the battle scene. Pistols drawn and primed, Trenchie suddenly ran down towards where the Cavaliers were making their defence. As he did so, he fired off shots in the direction of the Roundheads in their leather tunics and breastplates. "I think that guy is just addicted to fighting. Now what do we do? We can't just leave him here, he has already saved our lives."

The Cavaliers, with their hair grown long and some wearing their typical wide-brimmed hats, realised the incoming stranger was on their side and tried to aid him with 'covering fire'. Reaching their lines, Trenchie threw himself down behind a stone wall near the barn, gasping for breath.

"Be there William Trenchman amongst ye?" he shouted repeatedly.

The eighty or so defendants were too occupied with preparing for the enemy's onslaught to take notice. Trenchie crawled across the muddy ground to the body of a dead soldier nearby, still laying where he fell. Turning it over carefully, he looked at the face, which he was pleased not to recognise.

The drum beats of the approaching parliamentary troops grew louder as they approached the royalist positions, their 'colours' flapping in the breeze. Trenchie carefully peered through a hole in the wall to observe the scene. The lines of grim-faced Roundheads with pikes, others with muskets, marched towards them, with cannons to their rear. He estimated that he and his comrades were outnumbered by a ratio of about four to one.

The Cavaliers did have some mounted troops, but any charge against the ranks opposing them would have been a suicide mission. The cannon fire became more intense, but was not always accurate. Some did find its allotted target, such as an overturned cart used as a barricade. The wooden barrier was shattered; the two royalist soldiers who had been firing over it were instantly killed.

The opposing forces of the royalist Cavaliers of King Charles I and the Roundheads of the armies of parliament came face to face as the Roundheads tried to climb over the low walls and makeshift barricades. Smoke breathed from muskets as each side tried to gain the upper hand. The superiority in terms of numbers eventually led to a breach of the defensive positions.

Trenchie kept on shouting the name of 'William Trenchman' as he rushed amongst the combatants, stopping to shoot one Roundhead as he charged with his pike. The royalists fought fiercely, but were being overwhelmed by the attackers. A drummer sounded out the retreat – but rather too late, as there was no way they could safely disengage from the battle.

Some of the defenders turned and ran, only to be cut down as they fled. Others escaped into the countryside, while those already engaged in hand-to-hand combat kept on fighting. Trenchie realised that the situation was hopeless. He decided to fight his way out and get back to the churchyard where Jacob and Rachel were waiting.

"Who is it that calls my name?" shouted a royalist soldier in his thirties, following fast behind Trenchie.

"Trust me, just trust me – thou must get from this place… follow me!" exhorted Trenchie.

The way was blocked by three Roundheads, one mounted. Another one of Trenchie's pistol shots left just the two on foot to deal with. He aimed another pistol, which was unloaded, at one of them and with his free hand thrust his dagger. His comrade knocked the other to the ground with the butt of his musket as they ran.

"Trenchie, get down!" came the loud warning shout of Jacob, who was now in sight up in the churchyard.

A group of Roundheads had formed a line to the rear of the two fleeing men and had taken aim. The younger man reacted more quickly, shoving Trenchie, who lost his balance and fell. The crack of musket fire sounded, but only one shot found its target. William Trenchman fell onto the muddy ground, shot between the shoulder blades.

Trenchie crawled to the prone figure of the man who was his father. There were to be no last words – he was already dead. Trenchie, knowing he had to leave or join him in death, kissed his forehead before closing his eyelids with his fingers. There were more shots from behind, and the tormented old pirate took off to where Jacob and Rachel were hiding.

Standing together at the back of the now damaged building, they operated the time mechanisms, only to find themselves still stuck in 1643. "Into the woods!" urged Jacob, as they attempted their escape.

Unlike their previous encounter in 1554 with the yeoman soldiers in the churchyard, they managed to flee unhindered into the safety of the woodland beyond the fields. The Roundheads, satisfied by their victory, weren't too concerned about those who got away. Sometimes, pursuing a defeated enemy into woods could lead to a trap, and they deemed it unnecessary on this occasion.

In the safety of the maze of trees and shrubs, they stopped to rest. The ground was too wet to sit on, so they leaned against the trees drawing great gulps of air into their lungs.

"Can there be anything of greater sadness than the second death?" Trenchie lamented.

"Trenchie, are you okay?" asked Rachel, seeing that he clearly wasn't.

The pirate turned his head away, not wishing them to see the tears that had formed in his eyes. "To lose someone that thou hast loved, whom thou hast dreamt to see once more. Dreams make thee hope for what is not to be. Yet I saw once more, my dream became real and yet was taken away in a breath of wind. That man thou didst see die, he was my father, he died when I was thirteen. I had hoped that I could be his rescue – but I could do nothing. What can it mean?"

"We're sorry, Trenchie," said Rachel, putting a hand on the big man's shoulder. His poetic words were revealing to them a side of him which until then had been hidden.

Jacob ushered Rachel away to a place out of Trenchie's hearing. "Well, we're in the wrong time again, but it can't be a coincidence. The chances of us arriving at the very moment Trenchie's dad was here fighting, well… they must be close to zero.

"Not much seems to happen by chance, does it?" suggested Rachel. "We've been to 1554 and met the 'Martyrs'; now it's 1643, in the midst of the English Civil War. Perhaps, next time it will be 1687 – where your uncle is. I don't think it's that the time mechanisms aren't working; they're just not working according to the way we want them to. Whatever is going on, I just want to find your uncle and get home. I can't bear to see one more person get killed…"

Their conversation was interrupted by a loud cough from Trenchie, who was now ready to move on. "I have a duty I must see to. Ye can come with me if ye will, or rest here a while."

With that, he started walking on further into the woods, reloading his pistols as he did so. Jacob and Rachel looked at each other, knowing that they had to follow. As they walked amongst the trees, Jacob and Rachel often found themselves turning around and scanning the area. Every noise they heard made them wonder if there were soldiers about to break upon them.

"Where are we going, Trenchie – Godstone?" Jacob asked the sombre-looking pirate.

"Nay, I am making for East Grinstead to see the woman who bore me. It will be a strange thing to find her, and she to find her son of a greater age than her own."

"Rach, he mustn't meet his own mother... he can't," insisted Jacob.

"Why not? After all, he's just met his father, and it didn't change anything. The question is, how is she going to react? It's too much for anyone to take in."

From Crowhurst to East Grinstead was quite a long walk, about six miles as the crow flies. They were wary of encountering Roundhead soldiers who might recognise Trenchie. Avoiding the road, they made their way southwards until they came across a few stray Cavaliers on horseback on the outskirts of Lingfield. Grateful for Trenchie's involvement in the fighting, they offered to escort them safely through the then small town and onward to their destination. The royalists had some spare horses, with their riders no longer in need of them.

Jacob and Rachel learnt from them exactly why there had been a skirmish at Crowhurst. The large farmhouse opposite St. George's churchyard – home of the Old Tree – was part of the estate of a wealthy landowner called John Angell. Angell was a staunch supporter of King Charles I in his battle with the armies of parliament, and his troops had taken their fateful part in the conflict of that day. The South East of England had been a major parliamentary stronghold for the most part, although the royalists caused some uprisings and their troops managed to make temporary incursions into the region.

The soldiers remained quite stoical despite their defeat, believing that the King would surely somehow win in the end. Trenchie rode at the back of the group, unusually quiet, as if the events he had been through since meeting Jacob's uncle were finally taking their toll. Half a mile from East Grinstead, the soldiers stopped by a pond where they allowed their horses to have a well-deserved drink. A fallen tree offered a solid seat for half a dozen of the group, which they were glad to take advantage of.

"It is not good for us to enter the town," stated the most distinguished-looking of the Cavaliers. "There may be more of the enemy in that place. Therefore, we shall take our rest whilst you visit. We shall rest one hour; return within that time and you may ride back with us, if that is your desire."

Jacob and Rachel thanked the soldiers and followed Trenchie, who had already stridden off in the direction of the town. They made their way along the edges of the fields that surrounded it. In the distance, they could see the church and some of the timber-framed buildings in the High Street which were still in existence in their own time. They were surprised when Trenchie changed direction and headed towards a thatched farmhouse. It was not as grand as the manor houses of the seriously wealthy, but neither was it a hovel. It oozed charm, and Rachel thought how she would love to live in a house like this.

Trenchie ushered them behind a wild privet hedge, where they were hidden from the gaze of a smartly dressed woman who was washing cooking pots in a tub of water just to the rear of the house. She wore a green dress and looked elegant, but not so fussily adorned as would be impractical for her work on the farm.

"I have looked upon her not, since the age of sixteen years," said Trenchie, his voice betraying his emotion.

"Your mother?" enquired Rachel.

"Aye... my mother. The last time I left her in tears and now I have returned – again with sadness following. Yet I would rather it be I who brings it and not another."

Trenchie removed his pistols and dagger, took off his hat and walked slowly towards the house. She noticed him almost instantly, her work failing to distract her from the worry for her husband. Many times that day she had looked out across the fields, wondering and fearing.

"I thank thee for coming sir, but tell me plainly... is he dead?"

Trenchie found it hard to say the words. He had seen so much death, and been hardened by it, but this was different.

"Lady, he is."

Elisabeth Trenchman nodded and thanked him again. Behind her, five children made their way towards her – stopping short, not sure if they were right to be there at this moment. The oldest child, a girl of fourteen, held her hands to her mouth, tears falling down her cheeks.

"Children, be not afraid, but be strong. Father will not be coming home..." she gently spoke as she turned to face them.

The tears fell readily among the children except for the youngest, who did not understand. Trenchie couldn't help but look at a skinny boy whose thirteenth birthday it was. The boy put his arm around his mother hugging her tight, to comfort both her and himself.

Jacob and Rachel watched from behind the hedge, tears in their eyes also – the impact of the earlier fighting being stripped raw before them.

"Good lady, be wise about the future. Not all men are as good as he," warned Trenchie. "Some men..."

"Thank you, sir – but this is not the time for such words," she replied abruptly, concerned to be alone with her children.

"Of course," replied Trenchie, stopping himself from saying the things he really wanted to.

Giving the children one last look, he turned and walked back to where Jacob and Rachel were waiting. Passing them without a word, he set off again into the fields. Rachel exchanged a look of concern with Jacob as they followed silently behind – nothing needing to be said.

The two teenagers weren't sure of the way back, although it wasn't far. The woods beyond the cultivated fields all looked pretty much the same to them, but Trenchie always seemed to find his way, as if guided by an inner compass. As soon as the

Cavaliers saw them, they rose from their places of rest and began to mount up. The whole group had suffered from the traumatic events of the day – Trenchie more than any. Though Jacob and Rachel had not been involved in the fighting, the sight of battle was still a far cry from their ordinary lives, and quite a shock. The soldiers themselves, though battle-hardened, had seen some of their friends fall at Crowhurst – and that was something no one could experience without affect.

Henry Hoare, the highest-ranking of the soldiers, led them back towards Crowhurst. They stopped a few times to listen for the sound of enemy soldiers in the area. Hearing nothing, they continued until they had left the protection of the woods and entered the fields behind the church building and the old yew. It was then that a larger group of Roundhead cavalry broke out of their woodland cover to the south, yelling as they began their charge, swords outstretched in front of them. From behind the damaged church building, more Roundhead soldiers emerged, firing their muskets at will. One horse reared up, throwing its royalist rider to the ground. Another horseman, reaching for the downed soldier, found himself the victim of a musket ball.

Henry Hoare ordered his troop to divide into two groups and retreat. One group galloped back in the direction from which they had come, the other including Hoare and the three 'time sojourners' raced northwards. Jacob stared straight ahead as he rode, not even blinking. He focussed on nothing but the trees ahead. He was unaware that the Roundheads were gaining on him, but Rachel was not. Holding onto Jacob's waist and looking behind, she could see them. It was like a rerun of the chase at Foxe – but this time, for a reason they never found out, their pursuers abandoned the chase, allowing them to escape.

They kept riding until they were well away from danger, Henry Hoare signalling them to slow down to a halt. He was deeply frustrated at being separated from the other royalists, with the exception of the two remaining with him. "Be assured that we shall return and avenge this day. The banner of the King will one day be flown over this ground again," he declared confidently.

It was another one of those moments when Jacob felt torn between warning of how history would turn out and keeping his mouth shut. Thinking back to the time he and his uncle saw the soldiers returning from Dunkirk, he decided to keep quiet. The banner of the King would fly again, but not that of Charles I.

"Trenchie, are you ready to leave this time?" asked Rachel.

"Aye, if we can."

"Where do you want to go, Rach? It's too dangerous to go to the Old Tree," warned Jacob.

"The other old tree."

London and Paris may be rivals in terms of which is the greater of the two cities, but villages also have their own little rivalries. The village of Tandridge had its own ancient yew, and there was friendly debate as to which was the oldest, the one in their churchyard or the one in Crowhurst.

The three agreed to part company with Henry Hoare and his two remaining men and carry on. The Cavaliers tried to convince Trenchie to join them, having been impressed earlier by his qualities as a combatant. The pirate declined the invitation though, seeing his future elsewhere – and the soldiers rode off to face future battles.

"Trenchie, may I ask you something?" asked Jacob. "You fought for the royalists and yet you always seem to be against the 'King's men'. So why…?"

"Jake, not now," whispered an embarrassed Rachel.

"Fear not, lass – Trenchie likes an honest question. Sit down awhile, and I will tell thee my story. It is a story that has been too long hidden under a blanket of rum and ale – but my mind feels clearer now," the pirate said.

Jacob and Rachel made themselves as comfortable as they could, as Trenchie continued: "I was born not to life at sea, but to life on the farm. My mother taught us to read and write, we never went hungry, never faced hardship – until the war. The King and the parliament warred against each other. My father was for the rule of the Crown, but at first, in the army he was not. As time went on, he felt compelled to take his part – and it was at Crowhurst, fighting for his friend John Angell, that he met battle and was its victim."

"So you blamed the King for his death?" asked Rachel.

"Nay, child. I was but a boy when he died and hated the Roundheads for killing him. 'Twas my mother who taught us not to hate – and I forgave them, for if my father had not been killed, he himself would have killed another's father."

"I don't know if I could do that," remarked Jacob, wondering at the fate of his own parents.

"Three years passed and my mother married another. A royalist like my father but for that, not like him at all. It was not long before he showed his fearful temper, rages that would cause us all injure. It was in one such rage that I pushed him away from my mother, and in his drunkenness he fell to the bottom of the stairs. We stared at him as he lay; terrified of his anger when he arose – but arise he did not. Mother was afraid that I would hang and sent me away to the coast, where I could join a ship and be safe. I never saw my mother again, nor my brothers and sisters. It was he that caused my hatred of the King's men – he and those who have pursued me all my life…" Trenchie explained, bitterly.

"Trenchie, I don't know what to say. You're so different to the person I thought you were," confessed Rachel.

"I am a brawler, a drunken outlaw. This changes nothing. These memories of my kin are but demons to torment me," snapped Trenchie, his voice becoming angry as if to hide any signs of weakness. "We must go now. There is nothing here for me."

As if to dispel any thoughts that he was 'going soft', he removed the dagger from his belt, waving it around as he walked off purposefully in front of them.

"I don't think Trenchie's into counselling and sharing problems, Rach," said Jacob. "He's not the 'touchy-feely' type."

"No one's beyond redemption, Jake... and no one can earn it either," Rachel retorted, giving him a playful prod in the stomach.

The woods became denser, increasing their feeling of safety as they walked. Trenchie, despite his sometimes-wild behaviour, also offered the sense that everything would be all right, as long as they were with him. He seemed to be like the mythical cat with nine lives, always escaping the heat of battle unscathed and on top – if only by the narrowest of margins. This sense of safety around him could of course be misleading, as Manasseh for one had found out. The pirate himself was only too aware that with each new tale he could tell of escaping death's clutches, the odds for him avoiding the end of a sword or barrel of a musket were diminished.

Perhaps, the real reason that Jacob and Rachel felt safer around Trenchie was that they knew he was supposed to meet his end in 1687 – and they were in the civil war years some four decades earlier. The sad death of Trenchie's father and the eventual capture of Launder and Iveson were beginning to convince them that not only should the past not be changed, but that it could not. The conclusion they were reaching was that maybe they couldn't die there, as they weren't even going to be born until centuries in the future. Nevertheless, despite these positive ideas, they weren't intending to put them to the test – just in case.

It was getting dark by the time they started making their way up the hill to the churchyard in the village of Tandridge.

Suggestions why church buildings were often erected near ancient yews are varied and merely speculative. Still, the fact is that they were, and these trees remained a constant while lives began and ended around them. That constant made them useful for time travel. The old church buildings were also a fairly safe departure and arrival point. However, there was always the danger of building alterations and an unfortunate collision with a wall or pillar that they had not expected to be there – or even another person.

Jacob thought it somehow ironic that his uncle, who never went near a church building, had made their lives revolve around them by means of his time travel experiments. He felt quite an expert on these old landmarks now, even having witnessed how they changed over the years. He thought about all the people they had met, people who had been all but forgotten, except for the records of their names and dates, in his own time. It made him want to focus on what was really important in life, not just the pursuit of 'stuff' that he would ultimately leave behind.

Trenchie swung open the gate of the churchyard and strode into it. It was still just about light enough to see the mighty old yew that looked like it could stand forever – or even had been.

"Have you seen it before, Rach?" Jacob asked as he gazed at it in admiration.

"Yes, a friend of mine lives near here… will live near here."

Trenchie was now in possession of one of the time mechanisms and Rachel the other. Jacob wanted to try for 1687, where his uncle would be, but found himself outvoted. Rachel was desperate to see her parents, and she hoped that they could travel to the day she had left. Her concern was that even if they could get back home, it might be at a later date and that she and Jacob might be considered 'missing persons'. Trenchie just wanted a good rest in the more comfortable future – even he was getting a bit tired of all the fighting, and that was saying something.

Trenchie's wandering thoughts of peace and tranquillity vanished as the familiar sound of gunfire shattered the quiet.

"Get down!" shouted Jacob, as some Cavaliers tried to exact revenge on a group of Roundheads in the lane outside. Trenchie, finding himself wedged between the other two, didn't even bother to withdraw his pistols. Giving a loud sigh, he casually operated the mechanism's levers and buttons. He wasn't disappointed as the sounds of the skirmishing disappeared... and the darkness with it.

Chapter Thirteen

Peace in Our Time?

"Excuse me, but we were wondering what you were doing..."

The three time travellers were still lying face down as the elderly lady addressed them, her husband's face betraying his amusement. Rachel and Jacob couldn't help but laugh as they raised themselves up. They were too relieved to be back in their own time to feel any embarrassment, not that Trenchie ever felt any.

"We're actors practising for a play... we're trying to get into character," Jacob said with a grin.

"Oh how interesting, what play is it that you're in?" she asked.

Jacob looked at Rachel, who showed no sign of wanting to help him dig his way out of his hole – and then at Trenchie, who just wasn't interested. "Er... Treasure Island," he answered.

"It's lovely, isn't it, Peter, to see young people getting involved in the arts, not just hanging around," remarked the lady as they watched the three walk away down the road. "They even look the part."

"The bloke playing the pirate even smells the part," grunted her husband.

Rachel led them in the direction of a public footpath that

would lead them towards Godstone. She watched as a swallow darted low across the fields in search of food. It was a confirmation that they had arrived in summer – but in which year? She looked at the digits in the windows of her time mechanism, and with the excitement of a Eurovision winner, started jumping around and then gave Jacob and Trenchie a great hug.

"We're back – and it's the same day we left... well, the day I left, actually," beamed Rachel.

The burden of worry for her parents gone, she could now relax for the first time since she had walked to Jacob's house, oblivious to the fact that Trenchie, the intruder from another time, lay in wait.

The path took them down a hill, inbetween fields bordered with hedges and trees providing shade from the glare of the afternoon sun. Further ahead of them rose gentle wooded hills, a backdrop little changed by time.

They managed to persuade Trenchie that they should try to get out of sight behind the trees whenever they saw someone coming. Explaining away their dress and the pirate's weapons as 'getting into character' for a play wasn't something they wanted to do every time they encountered someone walking a dog.

"I am so glad to be back, I can hardly believe it," said Rachel as they strode along.

"Same here, but aren't we just back to square one? We still haven't found my uncle and we have to go do it all over again," remarked Jacob.

"I can't, Jake – not just yet anyway. I've seen things I wish I never had, and when I think of the people we've lost..."

"I know, Rach, but we've gone from 1554 to 1643, maybe next time we'll get to 1687 and my uncle. You don't have to go with me; I can go on my own. I'll be alright," Jacob insisted, not really wanting to go it alone.

They walked at a quick pace, keen to get back to

Wigglesworth Road for varying reasons. On completing the few miles to Godstone, Jacob led them to a field that ran along the far end of the gardens. It took a few minutes to work out which garden was which, as most of the houses were obscured by high trees, hedges or fencing. Fortunately, the professor's garden was quite easy to get into. They stepped over the low wire mesh fence and found themselves in the wooded area where Jacob had originally met Trenchie.

Number 87, Wigglesworth Road was a sight for sore eyes – like reaching 'Oz', but without the disappointment. There was one problem, albeit only a small one compared to what they recently had to deal with. The door key had been left behind in the house Rachel spent the night in, at the village of Foxe. Trenchie kindly offered to blow the lock of the door off, but Rachel gently persuaded him otherwise. Jacob ended up going next door, where a spare key was kept – his neighbours being quite bemused by his 16th century apparel.

Jacob found it rather weird to be back home with everything as it was. Even the milk bought the morning of the day they had left was still fresh. It was the kitchen where they spent the next half hour or so, eating anything that could be eaten straight away, without the need to be cooked. Feeling tired and thirsty, Trenchie tried drinking straight from the tap – until he realised it was the hot one.

"I wish you had a sister, Jake, then I could borrow her clothes. How am I going to explain being dressed like this?" laughed Rachel – not that she really cared that much, now that she was back at last.

After finishing their mishmash of a meal, Rachel went upstairs to the bathroom, had a shower and then went home. Although she had lost Jacob's door keys, her own had still been where she had left them, on the telephone table in the hall. She ran, not walked, to her front door. Disappointed that her parents were out, she was nonetheless glad for the opportunity to get changed before they returned. Rachel felt much better for having clean hair again and brushed it vigorously as she sat at her dressing table. It was the best she had felt since the strange experience in that place she called 'Encouragement'.

She had closed the door of her room, as if to shut out the entire trauma she had been through. The familiarity of the pictures, ornaments, and other decor was a real comfort. Her mum and dad had still not returned by the time she had finished getting ready, so she lay down on her bed to rest for a few minutes – the softness of the pillows a luxury. Those minutes had stretched to a few hours by the time she was woken by the shutting of the front door.

"Rachel, are you in?"

Rachel rushed down the stairs at the sound of her dad's voice, and on seeing him bringing in the shopping, she gave him a big hug.

"What's that for?" asked Mr Isaacson.

"Just to let you know I love you."

Rachel greeted her mum in the same manner when she came in from the car, followed by Rachel's sister Leah.

"Hi, I didn't know you were coming back from 'uni' today!" exclaimed Rachel.

"I told Mum and Dad to keep it a secret – besides, I wanted to see if you beat my exam results or not!"

Rachel had put a lot of effort into her studies, but with everything else that had been happening, she had even forgotten that the results were due.

"Don't worry about the results, love," reassured Mr Isaacson. "If you get the grades you want, that's great... but if not – you've tried your best and we'll still be just as proud. You can always retake them if you want anyway." He picked up an envelope from off the top of the bookshelf. "This came this morning, I was surprised that you didn't ask if it had arrived."

Rachel and Leah went to the lounge where they sat down on the sofa in anticipation. Actually, Rachel wasn't anxious at all. It seemed crazy to worry about exam results after what she had just been through. It was Leah who was the more excited of the two, as Rachel carefully opened the envelope and straightened out the papers within.

"Yes, she did it!" screamed Leah, as the results were revealed as one A grade and, most importantly, two at grade A*. Rachel had needed at least one of the passes at A* in order to go to any of the elite universities.

Mr and Mrs Isaacson, who were waiting nervously outside the door, came into the room to join the celebration. Immediately afterwards, Rachel was on the telephone to share the good news with other relatives and friends, but waiting to tell Jacob in person.

Back at number 87, Jacob and Trenchie had been fast asleep on the sofas. Trenchie had been used to a very active life, but since he had turned to smuggling, he had been taking things a bit easier. Much of the contraband goods were sold to innkeepers, and most times he and his gang would have long rests at the various stops – much to the chagrin of the local villagers. Smugglers such as he offered cut-price and sometimes hard-to-find merchandise from the continent. This was of some benefit to the poor, but it came at a price. The smugglers were often loud, abusive and violent. When they were around, the law-abiding folk kept their distance. It was always something of a relief to the locals when the gang moved on elsewhere. For Trenchie and others, this fear that surrounded them was a useful tool, preventing people from informing the authorities about their activities.

They were woken eventually by the ringing of the telephone. Jacob, feeling in a daze, somehow managed to find where he had left the phone just as the answering machine took the message. The call was from his uncle's university to remind the Professor of a meeting which he had previously agreed to attend that day. It was clear to Jacob that he needed to find his uncle quite soon – otherwise attention would be drawn to his absence.

The following morning, Jacob gave the house a good tidy-up – getting everything organised gave him a feeling of being in control, at least temporarily. He decided he had best open the mail that had come for his uncle. On finding various bills and correspondence from the university, he had further confirmation that time was not on his side – unless he went back in it. Despite the pressure to find his uncle, the time mechanisms, when they 'wanted' to work, offered the hope of redeeming the situation. They also provided the opportunity of escaping the present difficulties before the questions became too numerous and too awkward.

Jacob was keen to have Trenchie with him when he made his next attempt, the previous experiences proving the pirate a great ally. As much as he liked Rachel being with him, he decided that it would be best after all that they should secretly go without her. After all, he felt that it was he and his uncle that had got her unfairly messed up in all this in the first place.

Unfortunately for Jacob, like Rachel, Trenchie was in no mood for another foray into the past. Seeing the death of his father had affected him much more than he was willing to let on. It had brought about in him a real sense of foreboding that death was on his trail also. One more adventure could, he felt, be one too many. He genuinely felt a bond with his young companions, one that, since leaving home all those years before, he had only else shared with his old friend Collie. Besides, he felt he had more than done his bit for Jacob and Rachel, even if they had not found the Professor. In a way, Trenchie wasn't too sad that they hadn't. He felt the house was his now and he didn't want anyone, even Jacob's uncle, interfering with that.

The various technologies around the house, from the can opener to the computers, were still very much a novelty to the old pirate. Trenchie could appear crass and insensitive at times, but he was a better-educated man than he appeared or perhaps wished to show. His mother had taught him to read at a young age. Even when looting, in his pirate days, he would often take books and read them on the voyages. Most of his reading he had done out of the sight of others, as he considered it somehow detrimental to his wild ferocious image. Perhaps even he was in some way a victim of peer pressure – reading Chaucer and Shakespeare not being the done thing for a pirate.

He persuaded Jacob to teach him how to use the Internet, and the teenager was amazed at the speed the 17th century man seemed to absorb the information he was given. He did have a lot of trouble operating the 'mouse' at first, threatening to shoot it on one occasion. Jacob also needed to write down a list of very basic instructions, describing which buttons to press and when. However, Trenchie managed on his own much of the time, only occasionally calling for assistance. The old pirate seemed very determined to learn.

"It is a wondrous thing to read of the future, boy. Future to me at any rate," he said.

The phone rang again in the afternoon. Jacob didn't answer it, but deliberately let the answering machine do the work for him. The call was a follow-up to the previous day's message about a meeting, requesting the Professor to reply as soon as possible.

"Trenchie, will you go to 1687 again with me? You can have whatever you want, I just need to go there," asked Jacob, as the pirate's initiation into the world of computers continued.

"Have I not done enough, boy? It is not good for me to go back, and who is to say that the magic boxes will work again or not?"

Jacob couldn't blame him. It was true that Trenchie had saved their lives – but he hoped that he would change his mind after a few days. With people beginning to miss the Professor already, he made up his mind that if after a week no one agreed to accompany him, then he would go alone.

That evening, Jacob was invited around to the Isaacson's home to celebrate Rachel's exam success. They had ordered a Chinese take-away meal, as they preferred eating at home around the large oval table in their dining room.

Jacob had not seen Leah much, but enjoyed her company as they swapped jokes across the table. She was four years older than Rachel and about two inches shorter, at five foot six. He liked her bubbly character and ironic humour. Leah was not as outwardly attractive as her sister – but no less beautiful. The food was great and could only be surpassed by Indian cuisine, in Jacob's opinion. While trying to master his chopsticks, he wondered what Trenchie was doing, hoping he would have remained in the house. The thought of Trenchie going out with his belt full of pistols, which he insisted on wearing, was not a good one.

It was a lovely evening. Jacob was becoming very fond of the Isaacsons. Rachel's dad Bill was good fun, although his humour didn't always translate across the Atlantic. He would talk of his favourite NFL team, the Dallas Cowboys, and of their 'ups and downs'. Bill had grown up in Dallas before moving to Houston, where he worked for a number of years and had met Tira. After years trying to interest his daughters with no success, he seemed keen to unveil to Jacob's eyes the intricacies of American Football. Jacob didn't really get it – his only experience of live sport being an English football 'friendly' match between the local team, Crawley Town, and London 'giants', Charlton Athletic.

Tira, Rachel's mum, always seemed to have an interesting story from her journalistic days, or a strong viewpoint on whatever was happening in the news. She was well-travelled, as was Bill – but unlike her, he had never been to Ethiopia. Jacob asked many questions about that land, without explaining its link to his own parents. Tira had been to the city of Axum, where they had last been seen, and talked of its ancient history. It was believed by some to have once been the capital city of the legendary Queen of Sheba and the Axumite Empire, which had dominated the crossroads of Africa and Asia for almost a thousand years. Tira was pleased that Jacob found her stories so interesting, unaware of the reason for his fascination.

Rachel and Leah announced that they were to go to Cambridge for a few days to look around. Rachel had visited Leah there before, but now she had the qualifications needed for admission to the University, she wanted to look again with the perspective of living there. After the meal, they sat down in the lounge to watch a film together. Jacob offered to help with the washing up, but the Isaacsons wouldn't hear of it. The movie was perhaps a bit too much of a 'chick flick' for Jacob's liking, but he chivalrously endured it for the sake of his girlfriend. When it finally came to an end, Jacob thanked them for their hospitality before making his way home.

Unbeknown to Jacob, Trenchie had been spending much of the evening absorbing information concerning his own time; about people he knew and even about himself. The things he read online chilled him to the bone, followed by a smouldering anger and a desire to return again to 1687 – whatever the cost.

Jacob was relieved to find Trenchie still there and everything as it should be; less pleasing was another message from the university for his uncle. He listened to it, his frustration building with the situation, before removing the power cable and with it the answering machine's memory.

The following day saw Rachel and Leah travel by train to Cambridge as they had mentioned they would. They were able to stay in the house that Leah shared with some other students. It was quite small, but they had it almost to themselves, as it was outside term-time. Rachel wished Jacob could have gone with them, but understood it was too risky to leave Trenchie on his own in the house. Cambridge was somewhat larger than in Newton's day, as was the University itself – a number of new colleges having been added since then. It was now an attractive though smallish city, welcoming to tourists who could enjoy its long history and great architecture. The ramshackled dwellings inhabited by the poor in centuries past had long since been replaced.

Leah was studying archaeology at King's College, and she took her sister on a tour of it as well as the other historic buildings. Rachel's personal guided tour included Trinity College, entering in through the Great Gate to the sun-bathed Great Court. The thought of studying in such a place was really exciting – even more so when Rachel saw some of the paintings inside the Hall of those who had been there before. Among them she noticed such towering figures as Tennyson, Francis Bacon and, of course, Sir Isaac Newton.

A majestic beamed ceiling rose high above their heads and the wood panels on the walls. At one end hung a picture of King Henry VIII, not Rachel's favourite royal due to the way he treated his six wives.

"That's weird, look at that," remarked Leah.

"What is it?"

Leah knelt down to where a small inscription had been carefully and neatly carved at the very bottom of a wood panel where it met the floor. There were no others to be seen in the ornate surroundings, just this one dated 1687 – and bearing the name 'Professor Andrew Ketterley'. "The same name as Jacob's uncle, what are the chances of that?"

"He's not in Godstone, he's here," muttered Rachel.

"Sorry, I didn't catch that, what did you say?" asked Leah as she straightened herself up.

"I'm just going to give Jake a call, can I borrow your mobile?" Rachel replied.

Outside in the Great Court, Rachel called Jacob's home number – but it just kept ringing.

"While we're outside, I'd like to talk to Mum about something," said Leah, as her sister handed back the phone.

Leah had more success than Rachel, having her call answered immediately. Leah listened intently to their mother's worried voice, the tone and content of their conversation beginning to concern Rachel. Her fears were confirmed as the conversation ended, her sister putting a comforting hand on her shoulder.

"Rachel, try not to worry – I'm sure everything will be fine... but there are police vans outside Jake's house."

—⁂—

Jacob stopped in his tracks, having just walked around the corner towards Wigglesworth Road. He had only been gone little over an hour on a bus trip to the supermarket, now returning with bags full of groceries and a bottle of rum for his guest. He knew instantly the cause of the commotion. He had feared it would happen – and it had.

It was another one of those moments in life when you wish that you could turn back the clock just a bit, or done things slightly differently. Jacob wished he had taken Trenchie with him... or that Rachel was still there and one of them had gone shopping while the other stayed at number 87... or something.

The normally ever-so-quiet residential area was now the centre of something that would be talked about for years. All vehicle access was blocked off by police cars, and residents who lived near number 87 had left their homes. Armed police officers in flak jackets were in serious discussions about their strategy as they stood behind their vans for cover.

"Excuse me, sir, you can't go any further," came the polite but firm order from a regular unarmed policeman. The officer was standing with a crowd of residents who had gathered to watch the events from a safe distance.

"Jacob! Thank God you're okay." The unmistakable Texan accent belonged to Rachel's dad.

"Er… hi, Bill. Do you know what's going on?"

"Excuse me, sir," interrupted the policeman, "could you tell me, please, where you live?"

"Number eighty-seven… Wigglesworth Road."

On hearing that, he was taken to the other side of the road, and the policeman contacted the officer who appeared to be in control of the situation. A tough-looking armed cop made his way to where they were standing, seemingly calm as if the day's events were just 'par for the course.'

"Are you Jacob Ketterley?"

Jacob nodded.

"An armed man has been seen in your home. Is Professor Ketterley in the house?"

"No, he's travelling. I'm sure it must be some mistake. Who saw the armed man, and what did he look like?" asked Jacob, not knowing how he was going to get out of this one.

"It was a colleague from Professor Ketterley's university. Anyway, you wait here for the time being – I just needed to clarify whether there was anyone else in there."

Jacob rejoined the others and chatted to Mr Isaacson. As they spoke, he noticed a person in the crowd, who surely had to be the witness. "Hi, Professor Warind – what brings you down here?" Jacob asked him.

"Jacob – I'm glad you're safe. I came to see your uncle;

we've phoned him a number of times without a reply. He has missed a couple of very important meetings, which he himself had arranged. It's most unlike him – and now this. I do hope that he is unharmed."

"He's fine, he isn't in the house – he has just gone away for a few days. I'm sorry about the meetings, he's been under quite a bit of strain recently. Professor Warind, I was wondering if it was you who saw the intruder…"

"Ah, good, at least he is safe. Yes, it was me who saw the intruder – who scared the hell out of me, quite frankly. I rang the bell, but there was no answer. As I had driven quite a long way, I didn't want to give up too quickly. So, I walked 'round to the back of house and saw this oddly dressed fellow, holding some sort of gun and examining it. I don't know what he was doing – just admiring it, perhaps cleaning it, or loading it maybe. Then he saw me. He turned towards me still holding the gun – I thought I was going to be shot!"

"Perhaps you just imagined it."

The normally mild-mannered Professor Warind glared at Jacob, feeling quite insulted.

Inside the house, Trenchie was watching the scene from behind the net curtains. His pistols, which were trophies from past encounters, were loaded just in case. However, he was a bit confused as to why he seemed to be surrounded. He had seen movement in the wooded area at the back of the house and realised there was no easy escape. He concluded that, despite being centuries ahead of his own time, he was still wanted for his crimes.

"Long memories have the King's men… and the Queen's," he muttered to himself.

The telephone rang, but he ignored it – he didn't know how to operate it anyway. The answering machine, now reconnected, took the message, which came from the police – urging him to leave the house unarmed.

The police, having had no response, waited. There was no sign of anyone being in the house and as the day wore on, doubts arose as to the accuracy of Professor Warind's testimony. Jacob helped add to their doubts with comments such as, "Well, he is a bit eccentric…" and, "He has been overdoing it recently, you know."

It was late in the evening when the police finally made their move. Entering at speed, they broke in through the front and rear doors at the same time. However, after checking the house room by room, they found no one.

It was a bit embarrassing for the police and poor Professor Warind, who began to think that Jacob was right – and that he had imagined it after all. The local residents, fed up by now, were allowed to return to their homes, and Jacob was finally left alone at number 87. It was no mystery to him where the 'intruder' had gone. Clearly, Trenchie had time-travelled – but to when?

Rachel and Leah had cut their visit to Cambridge very short. There was no way they could have continued, knowing what was going on back at home. They had bought their railway tickets at Cambridge Station, shortly before receiving a call from their mum to let them know that Jacob was okay – but they still wanted to return home. Mr Isaacson picked them up at Oxted station and updated them on the strange events of the day. "Amazing, how a few wild comments can cause so much chaos," he remarked with a shake of the head.

Rachel went to number 87 as soon as they returned, to find out what really was going on. She hoped that Trenchie had somehow escaped without using the time mechanism. The other time mechanism was hidden safely in her bedroom, as she and Jacob hadn't considered it wise to leave them both in one place.

"Where's Trenchie?" came the question she had been longing to ask, as Jacob opened the door.

"He's gone… in time. He could be in any year."

"I hope he hasn't gone to 1687 – he'll be killed there!"

"We don't know that for sure – perhaps we can stop him, maybe the past can be changed a little. I don't think he'll be in 1687 anyway, why would he go there? He would more than likely just have travelled back a few weeks or even ahead if possible. The time mechanism hasn't allowed us into the future yet – but it has allowed him, and maybe again this time," Jacob said, exploring the possibilities.

They went into the kitchen where Jacob made them cups of tea before they settled down in the lounge to discuss what to do next.

"Jacob, I think I know where your uncle is. He's in Cambridge University… but in 1687. We found the name 'Professor Andrew Ketterley' etched in a wood panel."

Jacob slumped deep into the sofa with an elongated sigh of relief. "He's alright, wow – I feel like I can relax a bit at last. He must have got a job there. I wasn't sure how he'd cope in the past, but he'll probably be happy there. How about, we go to Cambridge with the other time mechanism and try to find him?"

"What about Trenchie? – he has saved our lives. Just suppose the time mechanism has taken him back to 1687; shouldn't we try and warn him that he and his gang will get ambushed?"

"Okay, we'll try and go to 1687 from the 'Old Tree' – to the date of Trenchie's death, if we can find it. If he's not there – and I doubt that he will be – then we can go to Cambridge, find my uncle and get out."

The plan seemed reasonable, as long as the time mechanism would take them to the correct date. The date itself, though, was in question… once Rachel had gone home, he went onto the Internet and tried to find it. The year 1687 seemed certain, but neither the day nor month was. In the morning, they drove to St. Nicolas' churchyard where they found Trenchie's headstone, emblazoned with the skull and crossbones, next to the path. It was old and worn, and the inscription could no longer be deciphered.

"Now what?" asked Rachel.

"Well, let's face it – we don't always arrive on the dates we put in anyway. Let's go to the 'Old Tree' and pick any date in 1687 and hope it takes us to the right day."

When they arrived in Crowhurst, they left the car opposite St. George's church and quietly made their way to the ancient yew. They were well prepared this time. They took with them a bag containing the clothing they had acquired in their last time travel; old money, some food, drink and other practical items. Remembering the dreadful ride to the village of Foxe in the bitterest of weather, Jacob also carried a couple of thick blankets – just in case they arrived in winter.

Rachel made certain that the year was set for 1687 before leaning against Jacob. She moved the little dials that altered the months and days without looking. Then, after checking that no one was observing them, she operated the time mechanism.

Again, it worked. The old yew tree seemed somewhat revitalized; the church steeple now appeared in its original form. The weather also changed. Sunny skies turned grey and mischievous; rain fell, but only gently. It was autumn. Wet leaves were sprinkled upon patches of long grass around the trees. Evergreens remaining so, while others hung on to the stubborn remnant of their foliage.

"Tell me it's 1687, Rach…"

"It's 1687, Jake!"

Chapter Fourteen

Lament for a Friend

At long last they had made it. They were better prepared as well this time, but for the absence of their gun-toting guardian.

"The weather's not great, but at least no one is trying to kill us," Jacob said philosophically.

They began the familiar country walk towards Godstone, the rain remaining light but constant. The ground underfoot was sticky with mud, suggesting that the weather had been this way for at least a few days. They draped the blankets around themselves and covered their heads, the damp atmosphere causing them to sneeze.

"Don't you miss the weather back in Texas?" asked Jacob as they trudged along.

"That's probably what I miss the most... and the beaches, although sometimes it can get too hot even for me. When we were in Houston, we would often take vacations along the coast – mostly at Galveston Island, Corpus Christi, or South Padre Island. The water's warm, there are loads of sandy beaches – you'd love it. We went back there last summer; you can come with us next time if you want."

"Sounds great..." Jacob replied as he looked at the clouds above, "we could take Trenchie and the time mechanism. You have your own historic pirate over there – Jean Lafitte. He and Trenchie would get on like a house on fire."

"Or shoot each other! Let's just hope we can find Trenchie again."

"He grows on you, doesn't he? I hated him at first, but there is more to him than meets the eye," he said, agreeing with her sentiment.

They were well pleased when they came within sight of the village. The White Hart inn could be seen opposite the horse pond, but it was by no means the only place for the traveller to find rest. Between them and the White Hart stood the 'Greyhound' inn, which was also a coach house, and the Bell, on the other side of the road.

"Where do you want to stay tonight, Rach?"

"Why don't I book a room in one inn and you in another. Let's see if we can find out any information about the Professor or Trenchie."

"Are you sure? Well, you better keep the time mechanism with you in case you meet anyone a bit 'dodgy' and need to make a quick exit."

They were still dressed in their normal clothes and used the shelter of a barn to get changed. The clothes they acquired in the time of the martyrs and Reverend Manasseh were of an older style to that of 1687, but were more appropriate than those they had been wearing. Rachel put on her dress, which had been dyed blue with woad and made up of a bodice and skirt. It was a bit like Cinderella before she met her 'Fairy Godmother'. For Jacob it was breeches and a common brown tunic made of coarse wool.

"How do I look?" said Rachel, giving her dress a twirl.

"You look good in anything – just don't leave me for some handsome prince. What about me?"

"You look like a peasant," Rachel answered after a thoughtful pause.

"Thanks a bunch."

Rachel decided on taking a room at the Greyhound, with Jacob opting for the Bell. He felt like trying a different inn after previously staying at the White Hart, but he was still connected to it. Unbeknown to Jacob, underground tunnels ran between the two. The plan was to have a meal, try to find out what they could and then meet up outside to exchange information. Following that, they would return to their respective inns for the night – where they would hopefully learn more.

Jacob passed a dappled grey horse that looked rather in need of grooming. It stood drinking at a trough, near the Bell, where it was tethered – it's rider no doubt somewhere inside relaxing. Entering the inn, he looked around, wondering whom to approach for information. He settled for an old man sitting alone in the corner, drinking ale and eating a plate of 'pottage' – a kind of stew.

"Excuse me, sir, may I join you? I'm a stranger here and am looking for some local knowledge."

The man was wearing a long black wig with thick curls tied at the back in a 'ponytail'. Wigs were very fashionable, perhaps more so now that King Louis XIV of France wore them and had appointed Royal wig makers. The man was neither royal nor helpful – seeming to be unwilling to talk. "I know nothing that would be of use. I keep myself to myself," he mumbled. Others in the inn seemed equally reluctant, peculiarly so – as if something had occurred recently that had 'spooked' them.

Rachel felt a little uncomfortable as she went into the Greyhound, wondering how people would react to her. She had been there before, but in her own time under its latest incarnation, the 'Godstone Hotel'. She wasn't sure if it was proper etiquette for a young woman to go to an inn on her own in 1687, especially an outsider. A number of guests gave her inquisitive looks, and she noticed a few people interrupting their conversations and pointing. Ignoring these, she ordered herself a coffee. Tea and coffee were very popular then – and haven't become any less so since. On this occasion, there was no coffee, but tea was offered.

Sitting down at a table, she felt more uncomfortable still and gazed out of the window next to her. A young woman about her age, wearing a linen hat, brought her the drink and a plate of bread and cheese that she had also requested. "Hope it is too thy liking, Miss," she said as she laid it down.

"Excuse me, may I ask you a question? I'm looking for some friends: Mr John Trenchman whom some people call 'Trenchie' and Mr Andrew Ketterley – do you know of them at all?

"I know not of them, Miss," she replied sharply.

"Well... Mr Trenchman is tall, has a beard and..."

"I know him not, Miss," she insisted and walked away.

It was an odd reaction to a polite question, and Rachel sensed that the woman knew more than she was willing to betray. When she had finished her simple meal, she tried asking a few others, but met a wall of silence whenever she mentioned the name 'Trenchman'.

Rachel left the inn to find Jacob, not wishing to stay any longer. He was already waiting for her outside in the road.

"Any luck?" he asked.

"No, none – the people in there seemed to be hiding something... or maybe it was just my imagination."

"I think you're right, they..." Jacob stopped as a child's voice called his name.

"Did you hear that?"

"Hear what?" queried Rachel.

They both heard the sounds of children laughing and playing. The noise seemed to be coming from somewhere behind the Bell, where there stood a farmhouse called 'La

Belle'. Jacob began to walk towards where the noise seemed to be coming from, with Rachel following close behind.

"Come on! The hour is late, we must go home," said a girl of about seven, standing on the grass outside La Belle.

"Wait, we have to let them know," insisted an older boy in the little group,

Rachel and Jacob stopped and stared as the group of children seemed to blur before their very eyes. This occurred several times before they came into full focus again, in the same manner they had witnessed with Launder and Iveson before.

Jacob was certain that they were the same children whom he had seen tapping on the window of the White Hart, but couldn't understand how that was possible. He had met them in 1554, and they were now in 1687 – one hundred and thirty three years later.

"Good evening, Miss Rachel," greeted the youngest girl.

"We are glad that Jacob found thee," said another.

Jacob felt totally 'freaked out', while Rachel, assuming that Jacob already knew them, just wondered who they were and why they had blurred.

"Time is short. The soldiers have come, and the people are afraid. Why dost thou not ask Reverend Butts where thine uncle may be found?" the oldest looking boy asked Jacob.

"Come on, come on, it's so late!" urged the seven year-old girl as she started to run past Jacob and Rachel. The others followed quickly behind.

"Don't go – please wait," called Jacob as he turned and began to run after them. As he set off after the children, he got to the corner of the Bell, only to find the road completely empty. Jacob had been no more than a couple of metres from the children when they had reached the corner, yet they had completely vanished.

"Where have they gone… are they hiding?" asked Rachel as she caught up with him and looked around.

"Where have they gone… and, more to the point – who are they?" added Jacob. "Do you know them?"

"No, I've never seen them before – and what did that girl mean by 'it's so late'?"

They obviously hadn't heard of 'Reverend Butts', but headed for the St. Nicholas' Church building, it being the most likely place to find him. Jacob explained, as they half walked and half ran, about his original meeting with the children and how they seemed to know who she was. Rachel tried not to think too much about it, leaving it in the back of her mind for now, along with the other mysterious experiences.

Light could be seen from the large arched windows of the ancient building, one again offering a welcoming glow and with it the confirmation that someone was there.

"It is a strange matter," Rachel and Jacob heard a voice saying as they entered through the main door, "but your arrival this day was preceded by a dream."

"Are ye 'time sojourners'?" continued Reverend Butts, whom they could now see near the altar.

"If you mean, from the future – then the answer is yes," answered Rachel.

"Careful what you say, Rachel – you could be accused of witchcraft," whispered Jacob.

"What happened in your dream, and what do you know about us?" Jacob questioned the cleric.

"I saw two figures in your likeness come to this house, and then I beheld: joy, sorrow and then joy, sorrow then joy and then great joy. The latter shall be, but not until many years have gone their way."

It wasn't the clearest of replies, but there was another immediate question that Jacob desperately needed answered. "Someone like us has already come here, a man named Andrew Ketterley…"

"Mr Ketterley, yes, and he remains. Do ye wish to see him?"

"Please… yes, please – we've been through so much. Can you take us to him now?" asked Jacob, almost begging.

Reverend Butts agreed. It was no ordinary situation, and he felt obliged to help as best he could. "I shall, but first pray tell, dost thou know of Esti Falasha-Mura?"

"I've never heard of it," said Jacob.

"Thy path shall cross with hers. Now come with me, and to Mr Ketterley shall I take you."

Just as Manasseh over a century before, Reverend Butts took Jacob, this time with Rachel, to the stables. At least now they were in no fear of arrest or of being observed. There were two horses there – one for Reverend Butts, and the other for Jacob and Rachel to share. Reverend Butts led the way at a gentle pace, whilst Jacob wished he could just gallop ahead. He feared that every second separating him from his uncle could allow something to occur that would prevent their meeting. The short journey seemed longer and slower than it actually was; such was his anticipation, until finally their destination came into sight.

"Thy journey is almost at an end, we are nigh unto the cottage. Hold thy peace until I say, so as to not disturb their little one."

On arrival at the cottage, Reverend Butts dismounted and knocked on the front door – gently at first, then increasingly louder until he heard sounds of movement within.

"Who be it that arrives here?" came a deep voice from behind the door.

"Be not troubled, Mr Knox – it is I, Reverend Butts."

The door was unbolted at once, and the three of them were welcomed in. Reverend Butts produced a couple of candles, knowing that the Knox family had none left, and promptly lit them.

"Welcome, friends," Mr Knox greeted Rachel and Jacob. He considered any friend of Reverend Butts' as a friend of his, whatever the hour or occasion.

"I am indeed sorry to disturb thee, Mr Knox – but my companions here with me are friends of Mr Ketterley's..."

"Then I understand thy visit. Make yourselves comfortable while I wake him." Jacob's uncle had been working with Mr Knox all day and gone to bed early.

The shutters over the windows were keeping out what was left of the evening light, as well as the chillingly cold air. The small door to the bedroom opened – and, in the glow of the candles, a slightly slimmer Professor Andrew Ketterley appeared. His face lit up as he saw Jacob, and they embraced in a long hug.

"I can't believe it... I thought I'd never see you again," sighed Jacob's uncle, tears falling down his cheeks. "And Rachel – you as well!" he exclaimed, drawing her into their embrace. It was tears all around and relief unlike any they had experienced – even after the escape at Lingfield. "How did you get the time mechanism out of my safe?" enquired the Professor.

"That was Rachel's work, she decoded it. I'm sorry we've been so long, we've been on a bit of a detour... to 1554 and 1643 – it's a long story," answered Jacob.

"Did you operate the time mechanism incorrectly?"

"No, it just took us to dates we didn't set, and on other occasions it wouldn't work at all. Sometimes it would blur before our eyes... even some of the people we met blurred. It's not just me – Rachel saw it too."

His uncle nodded, remembering the day he had seen the time mechanism blur just as he had reached to touch it. "I can't give any kind of scientific explanation for it, and I'm afraid that there are no guarantees it will let us return to our own time."

"Friends, it is good that you are here. Please now, sit down and eat with us," their host Mr Knox requested quietly, as not to wake little Charlotte. Poor as they were, there always seemed to be a pot with some soup, or a type of stew, ready to be heated up. Mrs Knox had now joined them and set about doing just that. She lit the fire, creating some welcome warmth – as well as greater light.

"That's very kind of you; we're sorry to put you to so much trouble – especially after waking you up," said Rachel, feeling slightly embarrassed – but also grateful, as she was still quite hungry.

They sat around the little wooden table as they ate the stew of potatoes and green vegetables seasoned with salt. It wasn't much, but it was warming to the stomach – and with the vibrant flames in the fireplace, the room was becoming almost too hot.

"We are not the only ones who have made this journey," the Professor announced to Jacob and Rachel. "Reverend Butts, as well as dear Mr and Mrs Knox here, have met an Ethiopian girl called Esti – also from our time, or close to it. They believe she is in danger, and they would like us to help them find her. I have also met Isaac Newton, and he requested the same."

"Wow – Isaac Newton," exclaimed Jacob – who was actually more interested in the link with Ethiopia.

"So that's why you were in Cambridge – I saw your name in the hall," added Rachel.

"I'm surprised it is still there. I wished to draw attention from someone in the future. I desperately hoped that one day time travel would be mastered and I could be plucked out of 1687 and returned. Did you try to find me in Cambridge?"

"No, we thought you would be alright in Cambridge for a while. The man who took your time mechanism, Trenchie – he came to our time and our house. He became friends, sort of, with Rachel and me," explained Jacob, feeling slightly embarrassed. "He saved our lives, and we were worried that he might have come back here, because he is supposed to die in Godstone – some time this year."

"Jacob, this 'Trenchie' is not some romantic Robin Hood type figure. He tried to kill me. He is nothing more than a seventeenth century 'chav' with psychopathic tendencies – and so are his accomplices."

"We're sorry, Professor Ketterley... Andrew, for what he did to you, but he's not quite like that," disagreed Rachel.

"Crime and punishment are taken very seriously in this time," stated the professor. "Your friend Trenchie knows that. He has probably lived longer than he would have expected anyway – besides, it is too late. I have already informed the authorities that he and his team of smugglers are on their way."

"Well, hopefully he is in a different time altogether," said Rachel.

"Nay, Miss, he was seen in the village only a few weeks ago," declared Mr Knox.

"But he left not long before us..." said Jacob.

"It makes no difference in time travel," reminded his uncle.

"I know he seems evil, but he did rescue us. We must try and warn him!" urged Jacob.

"Jacob, don't you see? He can't die yet because this is not how it happened. He was betrayed by his friend, Lieutenant Collins – 'Collie', in real life, and was killed in an ambush," explained Rachel. "The Professor has told the soldiers and that changes everything."

"Yes, if the history books are right – but suppose they're not. Come on, we have to find to him!"

Jacob rushed outside and mounted Reverend Butts' horse, riding away before anyone could stop him. As the others stood outside shouting at him to come back, Rachel mounted the second horse and followed him.

Jacob's horse galloped back the way they had come. The light was now beginning to fail, the moon half hidden by a sky that once again was blanketed in cloud. Dirty water was dispelled from puddles that littered the rutted track as the hooves beat down upon them. He leaned forward like a jockey on a racehorse hoping to gain precious extra seconds – not knowing when the smugglers would happen upon their fate. Jacob sensed that this was how it was meant to be – history to be altered and Trenchie saved. He felt no fear, but sheer exhilaration, as the horse stormed across the open country.

There was thunder in the distance, and the rain began to fall heavily. His woollen tunic didn't entirely protect him from the intensity of the elements, the driving rain making it hard for him to see as it washed his face. He rode past the Bay Pond and the White Hart, then the other inns and cottages until he was outside of the village. Jacob headed for Tilburstow Hill and his apparent destiny, wiping the rain from his eyes as he did so.

He rode fast, hoping to intercept the smugglers as they made the slow journey up the hill with their heavy wagons loaded with contraband. The towering trees on both sides made it immediately even darker, causing him to wonder momentarily whether or not he should slow down. Keeping up the pace, he continued until he approached the brow of the hill. He then eased the horse into a trot before reaching the steep decline.

He could hear sounds now, rising above the battering of the rain, which was beginning to ease off in its intensity. There was shouting and swearing, but of banter rather than argument, a number of different voices emanating from out of the dark. Jacob didn't fancy riding straight into a group of heavily armed and most likely drunken smugglers, so he dismounted. He tried to stop himself from coughing, the cold and wet increasingly affecting his chest. Taking the reins, he guided the animal up a bank and tied it to a tree. Slipping as he returned, he fell heavily and needed a half a minute or so to recover. He tentatively got back on his feet, his face and hands now muddy and grazed.

The smugglers were now almost in sight. Not sure how best to approach the task, he started calling out a warning: "Soldiers! – Trenchie, it's a trap!" He repeated the words over and over with increasing volume, his hands curved around his mouth like a funnel.

The smugglers went quiet, but there were other sounds now. Jacob could hear the noises of movement in the woods, the cracking of twigs and the squelching of mud. Jacob hoped it was just a fox or perhaps some deer. He kept perfectly still, not wishing to attract any attention. The movement suddenly increased and with all attempts at stealth abandoned, it became more than apparent what was happening – "Ambush!" he shouted at the top of his voice.

Jacob took cover in the roadside bushes as red-coated soldiers with black wide-brimmed hats left their hiding places, opening fire on the smugglers who returned it with their own. Flashes from muskets seemed to appear from all around, with some muskets failing to operate because of the ingress of rainwater. The smugglers had not reached the planned place of ambush when Jacob had let out his original warning cry, forcing the 'King's men' into an alternative plan of action. With the element of surprise denied to them, the difficulty of their mission was much increased.

Jacob moved through the bushes and trees, sometimes throwing himself down among the ferns, trying to get closer to the heart of the action. It was less cloudy now, the moonlight aiding him in making out the figures of the smugglers. They were more than a dozen in number, using their heavy wagons as protection. Initially, things went the way of the outlaws; those soldiers who charged along the road were cut down without mercy. Others in the King's pay remained in the cover of the trees, making themselves hard to hit.

As he got closer to the epicentre of the fighting, he could see Trenchie firing his pistols in the direction of the soldiers in the woods, barking out orders to his 'troops'. Jacob felt guilty as he looked at the bodies of soldiers in the road, now feeling unsure of the rightness of his actions. The smugglers, who had suffered no casualties, grew in confidence. Some left the relative safety of the wagons and entered the woodland, pressurising the soldiers' positions. The movement of the combatants now created a situation in which Jacob was caught in the crossfire. Face down on the ground, he could smell the foul 'eggy' odour of burnt gunpowder nearby.

Jacob's precarious situation ended not with his death, but with another marked movement in the positioning of the two sides. More red-coated soldiers were now advancing up the road to the rear of the smugglers and their wagon barricade. Volleys of musket balls flew at the smugglers' ranks, leaving two dead and others with wounds. The band of thieves, robbers and former military men tried in vain to hold off the attacks, now coming from all sides. Trenchie tried to rationalise their chances. As a group, they had no hope now that they were outnumbered and outgunned from the rear. Up the hill, the road was clear, but soldiers fired upon them from behind trees flanking it on both sides. The only option was to break out and scatter into the woods where more of their enemies lay in wait. He knew most of them wouldn't make it – but in the dark and with the cover of the trees, some might survive.

The sound of musket fire was all the while loud and unrelenting. Trenchie leapt away from the wagon with a shout of defiance and charged towards the trees. He was hit in the shoulder as he did so, not for the first time in his 'career'. The surviving remnant of smugglers duly followed his lead, the road now under the full control of the King's men.

Only six of the smugglers, including Trenchie, made it from the wagons into the woods. Those who had advanced into the woods earlier were already dead or dying. A few wounded smugglers fired off their last shots, tempting their enemy to finish them there, unwilling to face the noose later.

Trenchie hurtled through the woods. He had always been light on his feet, but he was no longer quite as fast as he used to be. Sporadic gunfire let him know that his comrades were falling one by one as he headed towards the Fox and Hounds inn. He had friends there and horses available to him; he only hoped that other members of his gang would make it there also.

"Trenchie!" called a familiar voice.

The old pirate stopped in his tracks and crouched down, breathing heavily as he looked around for his friend. "Collie, mate, most of the lads have fallen. Where hast thou been?"

Collie's voice was a welcome one. They'd been through so many tight scrapes – but this was the most challenging.

"It is a long story, and now is no time for its hearing. Now tell me, where art thou heading for?" enquired Collie, whose figure Trenchie could now just about see in the darkness.

"The Fox…" He stopped as they heard more loud bursts of musket fire close by – and screams that signalled the death throes of another accomplice.

"That was Davy. Trenchie, we must go – or with them die also."

Trenchie acknowledged his friend's advice with a pat on the back, before another voice changed his world.

"Collins! Return now, sir, or be considered an enemy," shouted one of the soldiers.

"You Judas… thou hast made a deal with them."

"I was to be hung – I had no choice. I am here to help thee."

The lights of flaming torches flickered in the wind as the woods were searched. "Over there!" called another red-coated musketeer, as the two smugglers were spotted. Collie started backing away from his 'friend' as Trenchie fired upon his tormentors, felling one but drawing more towards himself.

Trenchie fled further into the woods, but not before taking two more hits from muskets. He could feel that his shirt was now more soaked with blood than rain, his body wanting to collapse, but his iron will forced his unsteady legs onward.

"Hold your fire!" shouted Collie, causing confusion in the darkness – the soldiers believing it to be their officer's command.

It gave Trenchie enough time to get away, the lack of light making further pursuit more trouble than it was worth. The soldiers were happy to make their way back to the road alive. The planned ambush would have given them an easy night's work, but for the one who warned of their intentions.

"Lieutenant Collins, thou hast made an invaluable contribution this eve. But know, sir, that it is I who give the orders," came the stern voice of the officer in charge, Captain Kinsella.

Collie said nothing, fearing the reaction of the men around him – men who had lost good friends that night.

"Thou hast been spared a hanging," continued the captain, "and is this how my generosity is repaid? I will give thee the time it takes to reload to make thine escape."

Collie remained still for a few seconds as the Captain began to load his pistol – before realising what was to happen. He turned sharply away and desperately tried to scramble up the muddy bank and into the woods. Trenchie, who had stopped to rest, leaning against an oak tree, heard shots in the distance. He wondered who it was that was on the receiving end – and if he was now the lone survivor of his gang.

"Trenchie, it's us, Jacob and Rachel – we've got horses," came a whispered message from up ahead.

"Who are you?" replied the dying pirate, fumbling for his dagger.

The two teenagers appeared in front of him. Trenchie could not recognise their faces in the dark, but allowed them to walk him to a horse, his uninjured arm draped around Jacob's neck for support. He was heavy, weighing about sixteen stone on his six foot, two inch frame – a very big man for his time. The Fox and Hounds was nearby; the smugglers had actually passed it before the attack. They helped him mount Reverend Butts' black mare, Trenchie grimacing with the pain as they did so. They were worried that he would fall off, as they guided the horse behind them by its reins.

They approached the inn from the rear. The innkeeper had observed them from a window, and a few guests joined him outside to receive the injured man. They had been hearing all the fighting and had guessed what had happened. Smugglers often came through Godstone, and it was always going to be only a matter of time until an armed confrontation took place.

"It be old Trenchie... poor sod," whispered the innkeeper's wife.

"Let us help thee down, friend," offered another.

"It was Collie, he betrayed us... everyone was killed," Trenchie told the gathering in a rasping voice, as he tried to dismount.

Sets of hands reached out as Trenchie painfully lifted one leg over the saddle, the other foot in a stirrup as he eased himself down to the ground. He had lost a lot of blood and had little strength left, needing now to be supported on both sides. He was taken through the door of the inn and straight down the steps to the cellar, where a makeshift bed awaited him in the candlelight.

"Keep watch," the innkeeper ordered his sons, who dutifully went and stood outside the inn to watch for any sign of the 'King's men'.

Jacob and Rachel were allowed, after a few minutes, to climb down the steps to the cellar to say their goodbyes.

"I am grateful for what you have done for me this night," Trenchie said with as much of a smile as he could manage. "How did you come by my name?"

"Don't you recognise us? It's Jacob and Rachel... you saved us, Trenchie – we had to come back for you," answered Jacob, feeling helpless as the old pirate drifted towards his end.

"I know you not. As long as you are not 'Death', then I am happy," said Trenchie, his eyes half closed.

"We're not 'Death', Trenchie, we're from the future, can't you remember?"

Trenchie shook his head slowly and repeated his thanks before the two time travellers were ushered away.

Jacob and Rachel were consumed by emotion, trying to hold back tears. They hugged each other in silence for a time, having no particular desire to stay longer but neither to leave. They ended up waiting there for over an hour. The mood throughout the Fox and Hounds was a sombre one, people trickling in to bid the old rogue farewell. After an hour and a half, they decided to leave – there seeming to be no benefit in staying longer. They were also concerned for the Professor and the others.

The Professor, Reverend Butts, Mr, and Mrs Knox were very worried. The latter three had even begun to pray – much to the Professor's embarrassment. The Professor kept looking out of the window – not that he could see anything but the dark. He would wander out the front door from time to time, hoping to hear the sound of the horses return.

It was with great relief, on one of the many occasions he stepped outside, that he heard the approach of horses and the sound of talking. He couldn't recognise the voices at first, but then they became clear. "Jacob, over here!" he yelled.

They embraced as Jacob reached the cottage. Rachel went in and sat quietly next to Mrs Knox, who assured her that they were just glad that she and Jacob were safe.

"Trenchie's dead – well, at least he probably is by now. It really was his friend Collie who betrayed him," Jacob explained as they sat around the fire that had been blazing all night.

"Thou canst not change the past, friend – only learn from it," remarked Mrs Knox.

Morning brought the news they had expected... the smuggler and former pirate, John Edward Trenchman was dead. The village and those surrounding it were abuzz with talk of the previous night's 'battle'. Exaggeration and embellishment abounded. People suddenly seemed to acquire a link to the pirate, claiming to have been close acquaintances of the anti-hero. It was celebrity culture, 17th century style.

Some had mixed feelings. Many people remembered their own bad experiences with smugglers who would pass through the village, causing trouble at times. They were glad of the cheap goods, but not of their suppliers. Nonetheless, smugglers satisfied a demand, and everyone deserved some final dignity. It was decided that the pirate should be buried away from the churchyard, but nearby. There was a sizeable crowd gathered when the day of the funeral came. It even included a few soldiers out of uniform – and some old sailors, who according to rumours were former pirates... or perhaps not even 'former'.

A haunting lament was played by a young woman with a fiddle while the innkeeper from the 'Fox' beat a sombre rhythm on a drum. The coffin was carried by six sturdy men, the box draped in the black flag Trenchie had so often sailed under.

It was the same innkeeper who addressed the gathering. He seemed to know Trenchie quite well – even mentioning his childhood and the death of William Trenchman at Crowhurst. It was a moving occasion, bringing with it more questions than answers. Jacob and Rachel couldn't help but wonder what their time with Trenchie had all been about. Had it really made no difference?

How sad it was that the boy whom they had seen at his mother's side, back in time, had ended up like this.

The coffin was lowered into its prepared resting place beneath a willow, Trenchie's hat and guns thrown on top of it instead of flowers. Rachel, Jacob, and the Professor stood at the back of the crowd alongside Mr and Mrs Knox. Little Charlotte was well wrapped up as she was rocked in her mother's arms, unaware of the scene around her. The 'service' finally came to an end with a salute of musket fire – from some of the rather frightening looking 'old sailors'.

Some said it was a shame while others declared that it was the 'way he would have wanted to go'. Maybe it was – or perhaps the old pirate would have preferred to die at sea. Whatever his preference would have been, the choice was never to be his.

Chapter Fifteen

A Time to Weep
and a Time to Laugh

Thanks and goodbyes were exchanged at the Old Tree that autumn day in 1687. The Knox family had been good to the Professor during his time stranded there. The remaining money that Jacob and Rachel had brought with them was given to Mr and Mrs Knox as a token of their appreciation. The blankets and other items appropriate for the 17th century were also left behind. Reverend Butts gave to the Professor the items from the future that he had been keeping in the cellar. Rachel recognised her mobile phone, but said nothing at the time. The final exchange was that of weather – the grey skies of autumn for the blue skies of summer, as 1687 became 2011.

After the stresses of their travels to the past, when nothing ever seemed to be certain, a period of calm at last came to their lives. They spent the rest of the summer in quite a leisurely manner until it was time for the new academic year to begin. There were a few awkward questions to be answered when Jacob's uncle returned to the University, but not from Professor Warind, who was taking a few weeks off for 'rest' – on doctor's advice.

Rachel joined Leah at Cambridge University to begin the degree course she had so wanted to do. They were surprised though, to find the etched name of Professor Ketterley gone from the panel in the hall. The break from Godstone and its surroundings allowed her to push the unusual events to the back of her mind. In quieter moments, walking alongside the River Cam, they would often return though – tantalising her again with Launder and Iveson's enigmatic statements, as well as Reverend Butts' unusual dream.

Jacob also had tasks in hand, which helped bring him back to a sense of normality. It was an academic year that would culminate with his own A-level exams. A Saturday job at a wildlife centre helped provided some further distraction, as well as a small amount of money. Not surprisingly, his mind would drift back to their recent experiences – but more so to the possibility of more time journeys. The time mechanisms, or 'Kairos Boxes', as the mysterious 'Esti' would have called them, offered him the possibility, however small, to rescue his parents. When time permitted, he would devour books and articles on Ethiopia – focussing on Axum, where they were last seen.

Rachel and Jacob kept in regular contact, and she often came home with her sister for the weekends. They really looked forward to the Christmas break, when they could be together for a longer period. After what seemed like ages, it arrived.

Jacob treated Rachel to an Indian meal in Oxted on the first night of her return. Not the most romantic of places – but they made a good 'Lamb Pasanda' there.

"You know it's not over, don't you? I'm going to go to Axum – in Ethiopia. I have to at least try," Jacob said as he broke a poppadom.

Rachel nodded. She didn't want to so much as go near the time mechanisms ever again, but she understood.

"I think my uncle will come too, my mum was... is his sister. He hasn't mentioned it – I think he's worried about raising my hopes. It's a weird thought – rescuing my parents;

I don't have any memories of them. Sometimes I think I do, but then I realise they're just ideas my mind has cooked up, based on old film footage of them."

"I'll come with you, I promise... but please give me a little more time," she requested.

Outwardly, Christmas 2011 seemed just like Christmas 2010, but it wasn't – everything had changed. Professor Ketterley still worked hard, but now looked at life a bit differently. He had put a stop to 'burning the candle at both ends' and was now less certain about previous certainties. He kept the remaining time mechanism securely locked away in the safe – with a different combination.

One evening, while not burning the proverbial candle, the Professor tried to put right something that had made him feel guilty for a long while. "Jacob, could I have a word?" he called.

Jacob went down to the lounge, where his uncle sat in his favourite armchair, a newspaper on his lap.

"Jake, there is something I have to tell you – and I apologise in advance, but... I've been lying to you."

"What do you mean?" asked Jacob, feeling a slight dread – if a 'slight dread' is not a contradiction.

"I didn't get the time mechanisms in Antikythera during my holiday there. They had actually been in my possession since you were two years old. They were sent by Sonia... your mother... during your parents' stay in Ethiopia, when they were working on the documentary."

The Professor was worried that Jacob would be angry about being left in the dark – but he wasn't. He just wanted to know more.

"Why didn't you tell me earlier?"

"At first, I had no idea what they were myself. They were interesting, but I was busy at work and put them to one side. Then your parents went missing, and I had to fly to Ethiopia to collect you. With all that going on and problems in my marriage, the time mechanisms were the last thing on my mind," explained his uncle.

"Have you been using them all these years, without telling me?" questioned Jacob.

"No, no…" he insisted. "About a year after your parents' disappearance, I took the time mechanisms out of the safe in my old house in Bletchingley. I tried to find information about them, but found none. I couldn't understand what they were – I even wondered if they were a kind of ancient children's toy. I tried turning the dials and pulling the levers in many, many combinations – but nothing happened… until last year. One day, last year, I took them out of my safe and examined them again. Not for any particular reason, other than that I hadn't looked at them for a while… and I ended up in the time of the plague!"

"Nice one, Professor," laughed Jacob.

"Well, yes – it was a bit of an inauspicious first foray into time travel. When I returned, as I hastily managed to do, it was straight to the doctor's surgery for a check-up. Fortunately, I was fine, and from then onwards, things took an upward turn. I travelled to many different times, usually from a safe departure point such as the Old Tree. Everything went without a hitch, the only occasions it wouldn't allow me to travel were when I set a future date or a prehistoric one. It was when I was finally convinced of the safety of time-travel that I decided to tell you. Even then I was in 'two minds'."

"Honestly, you've got nothing to apologise for. You did what you thought was best," assured Jacob.

"Thank you, Jake. There is one other thing I never told you about though… a letter."

—⁂—

On Christmas Eve 2011, the Professor accompanied his nephew to the carol service. They went along with the Isaacsons; Rachel was already in the church building – again participating in the choir. As they made their way to the entrance, Bill Isaacson was surprised to see that someone had laid flowers beside the old headstone of the pirate, John Trenchman.

After finding a place to sit, Jacob's eyes wandered around the building's interior as he tried to make out which things had changed since his visits centuries ago. He did notice a brass plaque listing those who had served in leadership there, including the name of 'James Manasseh' and further down the list, 'Richard Butts'. "Oh, look – his first name was Richard," he pointed out to his uncle.

The first carol began, the candlelight so reminiscent of Jacob's initial meetings with Reverend Manasseh and Reverend Butts. The first reading was unusual for a carol service; it was from the Book of Ecclesiastes and was covered thousands of years later by the 'Byrds':

'To everything there is a season,
and a time to every purpose under the heaven:
A time to be born, and a time to die; a time to plant,
and a time to pluck up (that which) is planted…
A time to weep, and a time to laugh;
a time to mourn, and a time to dance…'

After the carol service, they made their way to the Isaacsons' house, where a buffet had been prepared for their return. It turned out to be a wonderful evening, one of those times that always stands deep in one's memory. It seemed almost perfect to Jacob, but missing just two people.

For that night, at least, thoughts about Axum could wait. One thing he had learnt from using the time mechanisms was that there was a time for everything. The mechanisms only worked at certain times, when they 'decided' – with no shadow of turning.

It occurred to Jacob, as he sat down with his beloved Rachel in the Isaacsons' lounge, that he had been right. There was more to life after all... and he would find it.

Chapter Sixteen

The Haunting

Jack Lewis put his spade down and looked into the hole, gauging its depth. Years of experience told him that it was of the correct dimensions. Matthew Henry was sitting down on the path just watching. He had done his share of the digging and was taking a breather.

The wet weather of the last few weeks had saturated the soil, their boots now caked with the clinging mud. It had been a particularly chilly autumn day; a powerful wind blew across the graveyard, making it feel colder still. Their workload had increased over the past couple of weeks, due mainly to the dramatic events at Tilburstow Hill. The fallen soldiers and smugglers had to be accommodated into their work schedule, the last being that of the pirate. He hadn't been allowed to be buried in 'consecrated ground' as some called it, but they still had been given the responsibility of the digging.

A thunderclap broke forth in the distance, causing them to glance upwards. The skies darkened overhead, as if to warn of more rain to come. "Will the rain ever cease?" lamented Jack in his world-weary tone.

"Not likely, but thou would'st miss it if it did."

"Old Mary reckons the bad weather was a sign of a darkness falling upon the village – and who is to say she was wrong?" Jack commented.

"I reckon 'Old Mary' drinks too much from the old bottle. There are no bad omens and portents – just men and muskets. Drunken smugglers, muskets and pistols... those three equal bad tidings, and there be no mystery to it," scoffed his younger friend.

"I have heard things here sometimes. Strange noises, but without a soul to be seen," Jack went on, as the thunder rumbled again.

"Noises... what kind of noises? Art thou trying to bring hellish fear upon me?"

As lightning flashed across the sky, a towering figure sprung out from behind them with a terrifying scream. The two men were so scared that they left their tools behind, fleeing towards the field beyond the churchyard. Stopping beneath the willow, they looked down at the fresh grave of the pirate, soaked by the rain which by now fell like a torrent.

"See what thou hast done? All that talk of voices!" bemoaned Matthew.

"It was only a prank, boy... I had never heard of such things. But, I believe we have seen the pirate come back for revenge – him or the Devil himself!"

Another clap of thunder sent them on their way home, via the 'Fox & Hounds' anyway – from where news of the ghost quickly spread.

"Mr Trenchman, what art thou trying to do?" asked Reverend Butts, as the old pirate returned through the main door of the church building with a broad smile on his face.

"Fulfilling history, sir..."

Reverend Butts blew out his cheeks as he wondered what was to become of his visitor. "We will be grateful if those poor men do not die of fright. It is not more than a week since they buried thee! Before thou wast playing thy prank, thou spokest to me of seeing the future..."

"I needed to tell another soul. For some reason I chose thee."

"Let me tell thee, that thou art not the first to glimpse future things. Two 'time sojourners' came in search of thee. It would appear that they found not thee, but a shadow of the past," explained Reverend Butts.

"Rachel and the lad, Jacob? Aye, how I wish that I had arrived back here sooner. In the future, knowledge abounds. I read much – even of my death and the part in it of that treacherous scoundrel Collie. It be a good thing for him that the time box denied my arrival until this day. Now tell me, does all this mean that I have been given two lives?"

"It does not, and may I ask – what wilt thou do now?"

The old pirate sighed as he thought about the possibilities. "It be the future for me, but in saying that, I might just hang around my old haunts awhile."

Trenchie returned to the doorway, gazing out across the open country. He reached inside his coat for the time mechanism, turned the dials with his fingers and watched the digits that offered him a choice of millennia.

"It is thy decision, Mr Trenchman, but I must warn thee: A man who is born once shall die twice, but the man who is born twice shall die once."

Baffled by the statement, Trenchie turned around as before his eyes, the figure of Reverend Butts appeared to blur…

For more information
and book orders,
visit

THE
KAIROS
BOXES

on the web:
www.godstone-novel.com

LaVergne, TN USA
08 April 2011
223475LV00001B/82/P